Fate's Apotheosis

Origins of the Exps

BOOK 1

By Alexander J. McCarty

Editor/Cover Designer:

Gabriel McCarty

ISBN 978-1-943733-12-5

Published by Sphere of Compassion, Inc.
https://sphereofcompassion.com
authoralexandermccarty@gmail.com
https://facebook.com/authoralexandermccarty (Updates daily)
http://www.instagram.com/gabriel_of_the_exps
http://www.instagram.com/sphere_of_compassion
https://twitter.com/of_the_Exps
https://www.tumblr.com/blog/sphereofcompassion

Front Cover design by

https://www.facebook.com/JefferyHerbert/

Ebui Sword Art
https://www.instagram.com/shiroyuuuuki/

Books from *Sphere of Compassion*

THE MAIN CHARACTER!
Hero's Epic Journey Arc
1. *The Hero's Epic Journey Begins*: The Main Character!

2. *The Hero's Epic Journey Continues*: The Main Character! (Fall 2019)

The Main Character: Legendary Origin Stories!
-1 *Guardian Angel:*

-2 *Broad Spectrum Assassin*: (December 2019)

OF THE EXPS
Rebellion Arc
1. *Exp 8*: Rebellion of the Exps

Resurrection Arc
2. *The Hero of Sel*: Resurrection of the Exps

3. *Sellum*: Resurrection of the Exps

4. *Destruction, Creation, Absence*: Resurrection of the Exps (Fall 2019)

Rise Arc
Eternal Rival: Rise of the Exps (Spring 2020)

Table of Contents

Part 1: Burden of a Shaman

Part 2: Gambling with the Gods

Part 3: Angel's Apotheosis

EXTRAS

<u>Acknowledgments</u>

This wouldn't have been possible without the continued support and help from my brother: Gabriel McCarty. We created this series and its characters together. He is always willing to help plan out scenes with me, brainstorm and brings these characters to life with his art.

       I also want to thank John Batchelor for all his writings on the Ainu culture. Most of the research materials I used are from his writings. Special thanks to Adrian Romero, who helped us decide to make Fate's backstory into a separate book.

       Also want to thank everyone who has helped us at conventions! Random Ramblings Productions is a YouTube group that we are proud to sponsor and they're super helpful at spreading the works of Sphere of Compassion. Robby, Monica, Riley, Chris, Oscar, Rosemi, Gus, and Adrian have also helped us set up and manage our booths at conventions. Extra shout-out to Jeffery Herbert who created the front cover art

       I thank my id for keeping me vital and driven, my ego for keeping me positive and critical about my work and my super ego for directing my creative energies toward a better world for all living beings.

Lastly, I thank you, the reader, for purchasing this book. I hope you enjoy it and continue to support me and my future books.

       Thank you! =(:3)*   (That's a bunny, by the way.)

EXTRA SPECIAL THANKS to our Patreon Subscribers:
Drew Markowitz (writer of The Planetoids; a fun sci-fi
fantasy animestyle novel series that blends Avtar style
characters with Miyazaki style worldbuilding); see link.
https://amzn.to/2XeyHru

Cameron Dicker (writer of the New Despair Danganronpa
Fanfiction: the most ambitious DR fanfiction ever created!)
read it here for FREE
https://www.wattpad.com/story/162152250-danganronpa-
a-new-despair

M. W. Arita (writer of Demi-Girl; an urban fantasy novel
that explores the mythos of Japan!); see link.
https://www.amazon.com/Soulbound-Scar-Fantasy-
Adventure-Demi-Girl-
ebook/dp/B07N8DJ5H7/ref=sr_1_1?keywords=demi+girl+
souldbound+scar&qid=1560791429&s=gateway&sr=8-1-
spell

Andrea Martin (talented artist who created the first Sphere
of Compassion fan art!); see link.
https://instagram.com/andy112138

Introduction

Of the Exps is a universe of characters, lore and stories! This universe is explored in a linear matter, except for the flash back section of each book which gives us a deeper look into the spotlighted character and their past. This is the first book dedicated to one of those flash backs.

Origins of The Exps will go more in depth with the backstory of various characters from the *Of The Exps* series.

I really hope you enjoy Fate's Apotheosis!

This book is dedicated to those who feel trapped by their own misfortune. I hope you find peace and seize your future!

PART 1: BURDEN OF A SHAMAN

Chapter 1: A Mother's Love

There were walls made of wood and a woman in a bed. A boy was crouched down next to the woman. Tears were dripping down his pale cheeks.

Not understanding what was happening, yet still perceptive to the emotions swirling in the room, I began to cry. I whined, wailed, whimpered and sobbed.

I felt as if the sounds I made were only perceivable to me. The woman in bed, my own mother, could not hear me. She could not feel my desire for her warmth. I was trapped and physically incapable of climbing out.

A man came into the room. I reached my hand through the bars of my cage but my presence was unknown to him. The man crouched down next to mother. He pulled out a piece of wood and began shaving it. Once he was done he placed the piece of shaved wood at the center of the room next to the burning wood. He began speaking to someone not present in a low voice.

At one point the boy let go of my mother's hand. He stood up and placed his hand on the man's shoulder. They both fell silent.

I continued to cry the rest of the night. My voice gave out before the sun came around.

That night I learned that the only one I can rely on is myself.

Time went on and after five years another woman came into my life. She was very kind and beautiful, but my brother never spoke a word to her. She taught me how to garden, cook, and embroider. Once I became of age, she decorated my face with sooty tattoos like hers. When I was with her, whether out in the fields or in the cabin, I quickly lost track of time. Before I knew it, two years had passed with us getting closer each day. But the closer I got to her, the more distant my brother became.

One morning I woke up and found her shivering. I fetched my father and tried to get my brother to come along, but to no avail.

An old man came in, along with my father. I had seen him before but only at a ceremony. This was the first time the aged man had come inside our home.

His beard was larger and greyer than father's. The flies buzzing around him and father mingled. Below his thick bushy eyebrows were very small eyes. There was something mystical about those dark brown eyes. They had seen things I doubt I could ever comprehend.

Father grabbed mother's hand and blew air on her to keep her spirit from leaving. "What deed has she done to deserve this? She has always been dutiful and loyal," he said, unaware that his hand was shaking.

"Has she made any enemies? This could very likely be the work of a witch," said the old man, searching through my mother's clothes for intentional cuts.

"A woman so kind cannot be despised. My first wife spoke out of turn, wandered from the cabin, and made enemies. She was an *amiyok-guru*! One time, in a fit of blind rage, she stole the offerings I placed at the altar, making me lose favor with the *kamui*. But this woman is nothing like her; she is calm, as rational as any man, and always courteous. She stays where she should and is always wary of danger," he said, sadness welling up in his eyes.

The old man crouched down to mother and pulled up her eyelids. "A curse has been placed upon her."

"It must have been that boy! He is so arrogant; risking his life and others for nothing other than his own ego! He takes after his mother, that's for sure!" yelled father.

"Brother wouldn't hurt her," I said softly.

"Not intentionally. But his ill will has manifested as a dark spirit and seized her. To think a boy could have the power to bind her spirit. Can this *uoitakushi* be undone?" asked father, sweat building up on his brow.

"I can only do what the chief *kamui* permits." The old man chanted by her bedside and made many *inao* as offerings.

I never once left mother's side for the three days of her illness. Brother never once came to the cabin during this time.

The third night the old man had succeeded in the exorcism. Father, him and I all rattled sticks around the cabin, scaring off the spirit that had possessed her.

My father gave thanks to the fire *kamui* and was in such an ecstatic state he rushed out of the cabin to give praise to every *kamui* he could find.

I confronted the old man as he turned to leave the cabin. "I want to help people. I want to banish evil *kamui*, like you do."

"You want to be a *tusu-guru*?" he asked with a toothy grin.

"Yes. More than anything. Please, teach me all that you know," I said, keeping my voice strong but hushed.

"I cannot teach you," he said, taking another step toward the exit.

"Is it because a woman cannot pray? I've felt the *kamui*'s presence many times. I'm as perceptive as a dog…just not all the time," I said, shuffling my feet.

"Women are fully capable of proper prayer and if you are as perceptive as you say, it is likely you would make a great *tusu-guru*. But teaching such things to a girl or woman is taboo. *Popke no okai un*," he said before walking out.

After approaching him many times a day for a few weeks, he finally spoke to me again.

"Sit down."

I nodded happily and sat down in the grass. "What's my first lesson?"

"I didn't say I would teach you. But I will tell you why I can't teach you. There is a reason that it is *hatto-an* for girls and women to perform rituals."

"And what is the reason?"

"They have no souls and thus their prayers are empty and lifeless," he said, staring into my eyes.

No souls? What? Every creature, land, air, and sea has a soul. Why wouldn't women?

"Haha. At least that's what I was told before."

"You, you're not a man?" I asked, my head a bit dizzy.

"Not entirely. As a boy I would dress up in my sister's *amip*. I related to girls more than boys. I prayed every night for the chief *kamui* to correct his one and only mistake: giving me the wrong body. I was such a presumptuous child. I did not understand that there is one supreme, perfect chief of the *kamui*. The *Kotan Kara Kamui* is the only *kamui* that exists outside the universe. He is the maker of all places and worlds. Any faults in the stars or misfortunes are the result of other *kamui* shirking their duties or misinterpreting his orders. I can't say I entirely hated being a boy; it allowed me to perform rituals and become a *tusu-guru*. If they knew I was really a feminine spirit in a masculine body, I likely would be banished. You won't tell anyone, right?" he asked with a wrinkled smile.

"Not a soul," I said, grabbing his hand.

I can't imagine how strange that must feel. Being born in the wrong body. How can his faith be so strong when his existence is in chaos?

"Good. Now, the other reason women and girls aren't taught is that, well, they are unable to understand the traditions of the ancients. They lack the mental fortitude and reason to perform proper rituals. Ah, the things men tell themselves," he said, looking up at the clouds.

"So then, you don't believe it?"

"I know it's false. I'm a girl in mind, though not in body. Despite this...malady, I am able to converse with the *kamui*, perform rituals and learn about the secrets of the other worlds. There is one last reason that *matnep* are not allowed to perform rituals or become *tusu-gurus*. Though, the men never speak of it outright."

"What is it?" I asked, scooting up closer.

"Fear. They fear nothing more than a spiteful woman. It is taboo to visit an *ainu moshiri*, but the danger is even greater if the grave belonged to a *matnep*. The idea of witches and the power of a woman's insults are evidence enough of their fear. They know that women are strong, and they want us to think we are *okirasap*. It's more than mere paranoia or a fear that we will make prayers of vengeance. They are scared of our virtuous nature. If a man prays for wine and his wife prays he gets none, who would the *kamui* listen too? Some believe that there was a time when both were allowed to pray, but the wise ancestors decided it was too dangerous. And they made this choice not without reason. Men are afraid that an empowered *matnep* can make them lose favor with the *kamui*. Give women the ability to pray and the whole system changes. And that, my dear, is why I can't teach you," he said with a smile before standing up.

"This is your chance to show them. If I'm a successful *tusu-guru*, you can prove that *matnep* are more than capable of interacting with the *kamui*. The one we pray to, most of all, is the undeniably feminine fire *kamui*—the divine *shongo-kuru-guru*."

"That is correct. After all, it is the *Abe-Kamui* who conjures up the entirety of our *ishu* and judges us accordingly."

"I never knew that. Please, you know so much. This is important. You can uplift all of us out of submission. Please, *ekashi*, I'll do whatever it takes."

He turned his head, only partially facing me. "Things aren't so simple. Customs do not change unless everyone in the village agrees to the change."

"Then we'll show them all. They'll have to admit that girls can become *tusu-gurus*."

"If they found out, I wouldn't be the only one punished. Don't throw away everything you have, my dear. It isn't worth it."

"We'll do it in secret!"

"Nothing is foolproof."

"You must teach me. If my daughter wants to become a *tusu-guru*, then she should be allowed to at least try. I'll take full blame for whatever happens. Even if I am expelled from the tribe, even if they force all the punishments on me, they can't say we aren't capable of interacting with the *kamui*."

Where did this sudden strength come from?

"Tomorrow morning, past that hill there is a cave under some vines…don't be late. *Popke no okai un*," he said before walking off.

We would meet in secret during the day, while the other girls took a rest from gardening. Only mother knew where I went. For nearly two years I learned all about medicine, rituals, and *kamui*. I was even given my own staff, topped with fox skulls, which was a special kind of guardian *kamui* called a *shiratki-kamui*. I was taught that the root of an *upcu* plant could cure heavy illness, that crushed dock seeds are for diarrhea, and that a heated nail against the tooth could cure a toothache. I learned there was a willful deity for every phenomenon in nature, each one complete in and of itself. There were male and female *kamuis* of good and evil and of war and peace. Distant beings that overshadow us, the *ehangeko-kamui*, had greater power and sanctity than the *ehange kamui*—the ones who lived with the land alongside us. Not only did my home have its own *kamui* that defended it, our whole village was kept safe by a protector *kamui*. Sure I was told all about *kamui* before, by my mother, but it was only surface knowledge. The stories Teacher told made apparent to me the power and personality of the many *kamuis* around and beyond us. Most of all, I learned that I love medicine, rituals, and all things mystical.

One day, a friend of mine, Hapuru, approached me and begged to come along, if only just once. I led her to the cave, careful not to leave any trace behind. Before the day's lesson began four men rushed into the cave. They seized my teacher and carried him back to the village. I called out to him in tears and raised my staff in retaliation. Teacher told me to lower my staff and was taken away. The next day, after a trial, Teacher was sent away from our village.

It was my fault he was banished.

16

Time seemed to lose meaning. Dig up soil, sow seeds, eat soup, go to bed, repeat, repeat, repeat. The daily gardening seemed more arduous and my time weaving, though peaceful, lacked any purpose. I would practice in secret what I already knew, but without a teacher I had hit a plateau. Eventually I even stopped honing my skills. After all, what purpose were they if I would never be permitted to use them?

A number of meaningless days later, I found a new passion. One of my mother's friends had fallen ill and mother had volunteered to tend to the baby. Seeing I was sad, she offered to let me hold it.

It was light and heavy all at once. It felt warm too.

I found such pleasure in holding the *aiai*, though I was still a kid myself. Despite it having no fathom of the world, or perhaps because it did not, the baby exuded profound joy. It was enough to get me out of my slump.

I found a new purpose.

"How do I make one?" I asked mother while petting the little miracle.

"You're much too young to be worried about such things, *apohonto*," she said with a smile.

"Can't be a shaman because I'm a girl and I can't be a mother because I'm a child. What can I do?" I asked, disturbing the baby with my negative energy.

"You can help me stitch your *akoro yupo*'s *amip*," she said with a peaceful smile.

"If her mother moves on to the next world, can we keep her?" I asked, poking the baby's belly.

"You shouldn't say such things. You'll invite dark spirits in. What we can do is tend to the little one so well that once she recovers, she'll let us watch over him from time to time."

"Then that's what I'll do." I picked up the *aiai* and embraced him. "Hmm. He seems a bit hungry." I lifted up my shirt and held him to my bosom.

"You'll make a wonderful mother," she said, holding up the patched up garment.

I feel something, but no milk is coming out.

"Am I doing it wrong?" I asked, switching nipples.

"You're doing fine. It's just that you're too young to make milk. Here, hand him to me," she said, outstretching her arms.

I stood up and carefully placed the baby in her arms. "How long before I can make milk?"

"After you've had a child," she said.

Of course! Milk is for babies. It only makes sense for it to come after I've had a child.

"I'm going out," I said.

"Don't wander off too far," she said with a wave.

I left home and rushed to where the boys always gathered. They were on a field, both boys and men, ten on each side. They were playing *karip-pashte*. One side had tossed the vine hoop and one of the more able-bodied boys caught the hoop with a well-timed spear throw. Since he succeeded, he went to the other team. Brother never liked this aspect of the game. He said it reinforces the idea that sides don't matter and could lead to future loyalty issues.

Time to look for a husband.

I overheard some of the drunken men talking about making babies with a woman.

If I want my own little miracle in the future, I should spend my time searching for the perfect husband.

I waited for the game to end and approached the most handsome boy of the group—the one who switched sides four times before the game's end. "Have your parents picked a wife for you?" I asked, moving my hips side to side in a bewitching way.

"No."

"Perfect." I grabbed his hand and smiled at him.

He pulled his hand away. "But I'm not going to marry an ugly girl like you."

Ugly.

He ran off with his friends.

I'm ugly.

I rushed back into the cabin, leaving a trail of tears behind.

Brother was in the midst of chanting at the eastern window but stopped once I had entered. "What happened?"

"Am I ugly?" I asked, trying to hold back more tears from coming out.

Brother stood up. "What's his name?"

"I don't know."

"You're too young to be worried about appearances."

"I can't be a *tusu-guru* and I can't have a baby yet. I really want a baby. And I need a boy for that, don't I?"

"You understand so little."

"I understand that I want an *aiai* and I'll do whatever it takes to get one," I said, standing up on my tiptoes.

"You'd die before it even came out. You're too weak to bear a child," he said with a cold gaze.

Why is he always so cruel to me?

"I'm stronger than you think!" I yelled.

"Then take me down, right now."

I rushed into him and pushed off the floor with all my strength. I couldn't get him to budge an inch.

Why am I so weak?

"I'm the strongest boy my age and you are five years younger than me. If you can't take down a man, there's no way you'll ever have the strength to bear a child. Now get to bed. I have to get up early to go hunting."

He went back to chanting to the fire *kamui*.

I didn't get much sleep that night.

The next two days I spent extra time in the garden, building up strength so I could one day be a mother.

Brother returned early in the morning on the third day.

Men and women gathered around him. In his arms was a fluffy creature, whining in a pained tone.

It was a bear.

Brother looked down at me. "You don't need to bear a child to be a mother," he said, handing me the animal.

It was heavier than a human baby, but it was also cuter.

"For me?" I asked, looking up at him with bewilderment.

"That's right. I'm entrusting you to look after him. You can name him too, if you'd like."

Brother smiled at me. Maybe he isn't as mean as I thought.

The little bear licked my face.

"I'll meet with you back home once I've shared our story," said my brother, turning from me to look at his fellow men.

I nodded and walked back home, making sure the ride was as smooth as possible for my little boy.

Once inside I cooked him up some soup and held up the cup.

The fluffy *aiai* lapped up the soup.

"You haven't eaten in a while, have you?" I asked, rubbing his little belly.

Once he was done with the soup, he began whining again. It all felt so familiar.

He's crying like I did the night she left. He misses his mother.

I grabbed him tightly and lowered us both onto my *aputki*. The mat was just barely big enough for the both of us.

"I'll be your mother," I said, kissing him at the center of his forehead.

He continued to whine and pawed at my shirt.

Of course.

I lifted my shirt and held him to my bosom.

He suckled for a bit before falling asleep in my arms.

I know what to call him! Noyuk! A good bear.

I woke up the next morning with Noyuk licking my face.

I licked him back and giggled.

How long has it been since I've had a good laugh?

"You should be more careful, *mataki*. He could bite you. Don't nurse him," said my brother, making a new *inao* with his hunting *chieikip*.

"But he misses his mother," I said.

Brother left the cabin without another word.

"Don't you want breakfast?" hollered mother.

I popped out of bed. "We do," I said, holding up my little boy.

"Here you go. Fresh rice soup for two," she said, setting down the cups.

Noyuk was so excited he knocked over the cup.

So cute. And he's mine.

I grabbed hold of him. "Be more careful next time," I said, before releasing him to enjoy his meal.

A year and a half passed by, filled with fun and fulfillment. Noyuk grew from a *peurep* into a *biyap*. But a little extra weight didn't get in our way. We were inseparable.

One day, I was playing with my friends. I had just tagged my *aiai* so it was his turn to chase us.

He leaped at the youngest girl of the group and knocked her down.

She screamed a wretched scream.

The men quickly came and pulled Noyuk off.

Her arm had twisted the wrong way and was now broken.

I rushed to my little one and wrapped my arms around him.

He really has gotten big.

The men left me with the bear and went together into the chief's *chisei*. When my brother came back from the hunt, a man whispered in his ear and he went with my *akoro-yupo* inside the chief's home.

I ventured to my friend's *chisei* and apologized to her mother.

"Get out! And keep your monster away from my *apohonto*," she said, holding her daughter's hand as the shaman examined the broken arm.

I left to my *chisei* with Noyuk.

After dinner, we went straight to bed.

When my brother came in he sat down by my bed. "*Chishirikirap*," he said, gently touching my hand.

Why was he apologizing? That isn't like him at all.

He then left to his corner and rested.

Mother kept watch over my *aiai* while I went out gardening. When I returned to the cabin during the shift change, he was gone.

Mother looked away, tears welling up in her eyes. "They took Noyuk. I'm so sorry."

I ran out of my home and into a growing crowd of villagers. I pushed through and found my *aiai*. He was trapped in a cage and crying.

He's alive.

My hands went between the bars and caressed his head.

"Let him out," I said with a fierce tone.

Brother put his hand on my shoulder and pulled me into an embrace. "*Chishirikirap*."

I socked him in the face. "How could you let this happen?"

"I need you to stay inside the cabin tonight. Please. You owe me at least this much," he said, lifting me off my feet.

"Let me go!" I yelled, slamming my fists against his chest. "I don't owe you anything!"

He kept silent till we were back in the cabin. He tossed me to the ground. "You killed my mother! If you were never born she would be here right now! You're going to stay inside like I said. Understood?"

I killed her?

"Understood!" he yelled.

I nodded, tears building up at the edges of my eyes.

He left me sobbing in the cabin.

I walked toward the door.

His malice bit me, causing me to nearly topple over.

He hates me.

It wasn't long before I heard cheering and singing.

I have to save my baby.

I slammed against the back door but it wouldn't budge.

Mother came up and hugged me. "Stay here tonight, *apohonto*. With me."

"What if that was me out there? What if I was the one in a cage, fearful and lonely?"

Mother was silent.

I put on a cloak and went to the *rorun-puyara*. "I'm going to save him. If the *kamui* curse me for exiting through this window, so be it." I climbed out of the eastern window and landed on my feet.

I ran past drunken men, some I recognized and other's I didn't.

These patterns. Are they from nearby tribes? Are they planning on sacrificing my aiai for this festival?

I had never seen the village so crowded. I slipped through the men until I made it to the center of the commotion.

Our shaman was crouched near Noyuk, his hand was on its head. He was asking for forgiveness. Pleading with my baby to not return with a vengeance.

My little boy looked so scared.

Two men opened the cage and wrapped a rope around my baby's neck and each foreleg. The other men sat in a circle around the fire.

"Horrible, isn't it? And all to gain favor with the *kamui*," said a voice behind me.

I turned around to see a boy around my age. The white pattern on his cloak revealed him to be from the Isepo tribe.

"Your people do the same?" I asked.

"Depends on what you mean by my people. I walk among them, but I am not one of them. Shamans exist on the fringe of society, not fully in this world or the other. Nice to meet you," he said, scratching his cheek.

"I'm Ebui. I'm a *tusu-guru* too," I said in a hushed voice.

"What?"

"Forget about that. Can you save my baby? Please. I'll do anything."

"I'm still in training. I'm not powerful enough to stop this."

The young people from my tribe and the neighboring tribes all stood up at once. They fired blunt arrows and shouted at my child as he was pulled along by a rope around his neck. Familiar faces all clapped their hands together, intoxicated by the excitement of the ritual.

Is this a nightmare?

"Do what you can!" I rushed in and placed my body over my child's back. Blunt arrows continued to fire.

I heard a loud shout.

Brother.

He ran up to me and yanked me off. "I told you to stay inside," he said, grabbing my ear.

26

The boy grabbed a dagger from one of the dunk men and started cutting at the rope. He was soon lifted off his feet.

Two men stood up and grabbed my son's hindquarters and face. A third man went up to my *aiai*. He was holding a piece of wood.

"Stop!" I screamed.

The boy slammed his knee into the teeth of the man holding him. He squeezed out from the man's grip and went back to cutting the rope.

Once it broke, he was pinned down by two men.

"Run!" I yelled to my baby.

Noyuk clawed at the man trying to shove a piece of wood in its mouth.

I slipped out of my brother's grip and pierced a man with his own dagger.

"Ay-oh!" he screamed. The man released my baby's mouth, but two men behind were still strangling my little one with a rope knotted into a noose.

He's almost free.

"Get out of here!" I yelled.

The man I hurt raised his hand to strike me, but my *akoro yupo* gripped his wrist. Brother pulled a bow out from his quiver and pierced it through my baby's head.

My little one was dead in an instant.

This can't be real.

Brother grabbed me and carried me off.

My baby is dead. He's dead.

Through the drunken men and shadowy faces, I was carried back home. Brother set me down on my bed.

My whole body was shaking.

Noyuk is really gone.

"Get some rest," he said.

"Why does the chief *kamui* hate me?" I asked, tears racing down my cheeks.

I'm cursed.

"He doesn't hate anyone. You're being conceited."

"You killed my *aiai*!" I yelled, grabbing whatever I could find and launching it at him.

"And you killed my mother!" he yelled before storming out of the *chisei*.

"Mother! Where are you?" I went to her corner but she wasn't there.

I'm not leaving. I'll guard this place like a ghost and attack anyone who enters.

The next three days sapped my essence like a curse. I blocked the doors and threatened to kill anyone who entered. Brother eventually broke through and disarmed me. I cried myself to sleep that night. When mother came back the following morning, I sobbed in her arms. But even her embrace lost its warmth. After all, how long would it be before my curse took her life? On the third day, the oldest woman of the village passed on. Brother forced me into clothes and dragged me along; all the while I spouted all the curses I could think of.

I was supposed to weep with the other girls, but I didn't know the woman who had gone away. The men were solemn too. But who cares? These men and the women too, they were all there when my *aiai* was killed.

They are all responsible. They all deserve my wrath.

I mouthed curses to each one but it felt ineffectual. As far as I was concerned, they should all die.

I should die too.

I overheard a couple muttering about the resting old woman in their *chisei*. The *paunguru* prohibited them to enter and said that it would be burned down. The couple asked if they could get their belongings out, but the chief outright refused them.

"The ghosts of old women are especially deadly. If you enter that cabin you not only put your life and that of your families at risk, you risk dooming our entire village to her wrath."

Doom the entire village.

The couple nodded and left with their neighbors to their home.

"When is it to be burned down?" asked my brother.

"As soon as possible," said the chief.

I better hurry. An opportunity like this won't come again. None of us deserve to live. We all deserve death.

Chapter 2: Taboo

As soon as the funeral service ended, I ran off to find the cabin where the old woman had gone away. Upon arrival, I felt a shift in air pressure. She was here alright, and she was very powerful.

I need to get her upset, really upset.

I stomped my way around the cabin and kicked open the front door.

Her presence built up at my feet, but I kept moving.

I grabbed a club from the man's corner and smashed everything I could find.

"That old woman was a total nuisance. Her funeral felt more like a celebration than a ceremony of loss. We all took turns talking about how she made our lives more difficult."

A powerful wind swirled inside, knocking over the *inao* placed by the eastern window.

"They say this place is haunted, but that weak old woman could never have the power to curse someone."

I smelled something…*shupuya.*

That was fast. Better finish up.

The front door slammed shut by a powerful gust.

"It sure is windy today," I said before spitting at the holy altar.

If her wrath isn't sufficient, then enraging the kamui should get the desired result.

"You feel that heat? That's a fire. They are going to burn this place so you'll have nowhere to go. We don't want you anymore so just leave us alone!"

I turned to the sacred east window. It was now blocked by a tower of flames.

Okay, back exit.

I slammed against the back door, but a force greater than my own kept it closed.

Please let the front be open.

I rammed my body into the front door. It didn't budge.

Bad. This is very bad.

"You may take my life! But what about the others! They all mock you! They all hate you! They are burning down your residence and there is nothing you can do!" I yelled as loud as I could.

I deserve to die. This is only fair. It's so hot, but I can't stop shivering.

"Do your worst!"

Maybe this is for the best. If her hex is insufficient, I'll haunt them all till they die of illness. I'll end the whole village with my motherly wrath.

"Go ahead and burn me!"

I heard something slam into the door.

The middle portion of the door burst open.

"Get out of here now!" yelled my brother.

"No! I'm going to burn and it's all your fault! This is what you get for killing my baby!"

31

He squeezed through the broken door, slicing his legs in the process.

"What do you care if I die? I killed your mother, didn't I? You hate me! Well I hate you too!"

I hate everyone.

Brother tore off my shirt and tossed it into the flames. He lifted me up and held me to his chest, shielding me from the heat.

He squeezed through the door once more, which now had fire brewing at its bottom.

As soon as we got out, my brother brought me to the shaman's home.

"You are more wounded than she is," said the *tusu-guru*.

"Forget the wounds. My sister was possessed. A *nitnep* took over her," said my brother.

A man rushed into the cabin. "Is she okay?"

Father had returned from his fight with the Horokeu tribe.

"She has been possessed by snakes, father," said my brother.

"The *paunguru* has called for a meeting to discuss her punishment. What did she do?" asked father, examining the wounds on my brother's legs.

"A spirit possessed her to enter another spirit's domain. Foolish sister, you will be made infertile by the ghost's curse," he said, chewing burdock leaves before applying the salve to the burn marks on my arms.

Even now he mocks me. I hate him.

"How can I bring a child into a world that raises animals only to kill them? He was my baby!" I yelled, hitting my brother.

32

Father seized my head and ran his hand down the length of my hair from my crown to my shoulders. "There, there, *apohonto*. You were a splendid mother. I am so very proud of you."

I never meant to bring him into this. Please let father be safe from my curse.

"You're praising her after what she's done!" yelled my brother.

"You had her take care of a *hepere*? What were you thinking?" asked father, still stroking me.

"I didn't know she would get so attached. Children tend to play with the cubs and women nurture them, but never has anyone tried to stop the ceremony."

"You killed his mother, brought him to me only to kill him yourself. Why must you torment me? Is it because I killed your mother?" I asked, held down by the shaman.

"The fire *kamui* shirked her duties. It was not your fault she is sleeping," said father in a hushed tone.

The shaman turned to my brother. "Ebui is not possessed. What your sister did, she did of her own accord."

"And so her mother's madness finally shows itself. I will stay with her while she heals. Do your best to mitigate her punishment," said father, looking at my brother while crouching down next to me.

The shaman and my brother left the cabin.

"That boy has caused you great harm, but you must stay *okira*," said father, moving a clump of my hair back.

Father is always so strong. He has truly lived up to his name.

"You wouldn't have let them kill my *aiai*, would you?" I asked, starting to tear up.

"Traditions only change by a unanimous vote. I alone can change nothing. I follow the *tuitak*, traditions and customs. I pray daily and with sincerity. When I am called to battle, I fight to protect the village. You cannot change things, *apohonto*. You must simply adjust and move on. If it were up to me, you never would have spent time with that bear cub. To go through such a loss at your age—it isn't right."

"What isn't right is killing someone you know."

"Then killing a stranger is okay?"

"That's not what I meant. Noyuk was my baby. I loved him so much."

"And I'm sure you'll make a wonderful mother."

"I'm done with that. I'm done with love and magic! I'm sick of this village and everyone in it!"

I should have died in that chisei, *surrounded by flames.*

"Get some rest, *apohonto*."

"Yeah, I am pretty tired." I closed my eyes and fell asleep.

When I awoke, it was early morning and a shirt was placed on me.

Brother was looming over me. "Get up."

I turned away from him as I slipped into the new shirt.

"What did they decide, Akno?" asked father, holding mother's hand.

Brother gritted his teeth. "Banishment."

What?

"Let me talk to the *paunguru*," said father, getting up from the floor.

"I packed your things, *mataki*," said my brother, putting my *korobe* into a single pile.

"Where am I going?" I asked.

"Away from here. And you can't return."

I've been banished?

"Calm down. Okira is talking with the chief. I'm sure things will work out. Ebui is only a child," said mother.

"The chief knows she purposefully went into that home. Your little bud tried to curse all of us," said my brother, glaring at mother.

"But how will she survive on her own?" asked mother, her eyes becoming wet.

I never meant to hurt her.

"I'll be okay. Teacher taught me what is poisonous and edible. I'll be fine," I said, embracing my mother with all my love.

I may never hug her again.

"*Mataki*, it's time." Brother attached all my things to a *tara*, fastened it around my lower back and led me out of the cabin.

Father was shouting at the *paunguru*.

I waved at him.

Father rushed over to me.

No words were exchanged. He embraced me one last time.

Brother and father led me to the edge of the village.

"Stay safe. *Sarampa*," said father, forcing a smile.

"Keep searching for a village that will accept you. Be respectful of your new family. *Sarampa*," said my brother.

I walked past the village borders and entered the forest.

This wasn't supposed to happen.

Four days and nights passed without any soup and without the safety of a *chisei*. It rained on the fourth night and the trees provided less shelter than I had hoped. I woke up shivering throughout that night. On the fifth morning, I came across a man, but he had no pattern on his shirt from which to identify his tribe.

What if he's an enemy?

"Who's there?" he asked, holding up his bow and arrow.

If I move, he may shoot on reflex. Don't have many options.

"I'm just a girl. I'm not armed," I said, coming out of the bushes with my hands raised.

The man lowered his weapon and walked up to me. "You're shivering. Come with me. The *tusu-guru* from my village will heal you," he said, placing his shirt over my shoulders.

"What village are you from?" I asked while following him.

"What about you?"

I stood up proud. "Shitumbe."

"Where you banished as well?"

"What makes you say that?"

"You're either lost or banished. There's no need to be ashamed. I was picked up around here when I was kicked out of my village. I was once a Horokeu."

He's our enemy.

I stopped in place. "What did you do?"

"Relax. I'm not going to hurt you. My friend stole some things and got caught. I took the blame for him. He wasn't well liked. The incident would have likely resulted in a severe punishment for him."

"The Horokeu have friends? I thought they were savages, like the *koropok-gurus*."

"Even savages have friends."

"Then you don't eat *ainu*?"

"Is that what your people told you? We may be ruthless in battle, but otherwise we aren't all that *uoaya* from you, *furep*."

"It's Shitumbe," I said, holding my head up high.

"Not anymore. You aren't a fox and I'm no longer a wolf. We're just Ainu," he said with a smile.

He's wrong. Banished or not, I'm a Shitumbe.

I followed him all the way to his village and gave him back his shirt once my shivering died down. The village was small, consisting of twenty-two homes, all the same size. As we walked by, I peeked inside, seeing as many as six people per house.

"Do you have a leader?" I asked, covering my red pattern as best I could as their eyes judged me.

"We have a *nupuru-guru* who helped establish this place. His name is Hechaka. And he's aptly named. He cleared the fog away from so many of us." The man who was once a Horokeu opened the door to a *chisei*.

It's him!

The one who inspired me, who helped me find my purpose, was seated on a mat in front of me. He was wearing a blend of shamanic garb and women's clothing. He even had a headdress now. The twinkle in his eye meant he recognized me.

My teacher's smile faded as he stood up. "Why were you banished?"

"It's really you." My mind went blank and all of a sudden I was hugging him. He was more than a familiar face; he was my teacher. Once I came to my senses, I immediately broke out of the hug. "My apologies. I meant no disrespect."

I can't be seen as a child.

"No need for concern. We do not have the same customs here," said Teacher, showing me the beads in his hair and tapping his now shaved chin. "Lie down. You're still shaking," said Hechaka with a smile.

"Wait. If the customs are different…can you teach me? I want to be a *tusu-guru*! I want to talk with the *kamui*, lose myself in a divination, and help people heal!"

"If you are here, then there is surely a reason behind it. This is the place where those without a destiny can forge a new future. You sent me on this path and now you have come upon the path you brought about. Our destinies are linked, Ebui. I will share with you all I know. Once you get over your sickness, that is," he said, gesturing for me to lie down.

Thirty-two days later, an outsider was brought into our village.

As the shaman's apprentice, it was my duty to assist in tending to the outsider's wounds. Upon entering the cabin, I found a boy. It was the same boy who tried to help me save my baby.

Did destiny bring him here?

"Hold onto his hand; we mustn't let his spirit leave. Check his body for wounds," said Hechaka, pulling her hand away from the boy's heated forehead.

I gripped the boy's hand and examined him. I found blood stains on the edges of his shirt but saw no wound on his body.

Where did the blood come from?

"Take a look into his eyes. What is your assessment?"

I lifted up his eyelids. They were a nice amber color. "They are heavily dilated. Shall I ask the fire *kamui* to heal him?"

"No. Keep him calm. Make sure his spirit does not leave his body. I will call upon a powerful *kamui* in the meantime."

"I know he has a fever, but do you really think that is necessary?"

"It is."

"Should I bring you some rice wine?"

"A possession cannot be forced. One must make their mind receptive through prayer and contemplation. This is likely your first time witnessing a possession. Worry not; you will be in no danger." Teacher sat down on her knees and faced the eastern window. She chanted beneath her breath.

I took in a deep breath and centered my mind on joy.

"♫ The bunny gets lost in the rain. Lost in the rain.

He is scared, he is hurt, and he is cold.

He was lost in the rain. Lost in the rain.

Spent days searching for his home.

Then one day, when the sun was shining and the rain had cleared,

a fox came by. A fox, oh my.

The fox bared his teeth and the bunny cried. The bunny ran, afraid to die.

But the fox was fast, oh so fast.

He jumped on the bunny. Jumped on the bunny.

He bared his teeth, once again.

Then asked if the bunny would be his friend.

The bunny stood up. Up. Up. Up.

He licked the fox's face with friendly love.

He thought he was lost, but now he was found.

If it rained or snowed. Whether warm or cold.

With a snuggle and love. A kiss and hug.

The fox would always guide him home.

The bunny was lost. Lost in the rain.

But the fox would always guide him home. ♫"

Singing the story my mother used to relax me ended up bringing back an intense longing for home.

I want to see her…and father too.

Teacher's eyes slowly opened. Her spine contorted and she leaned over the boy. "Dark spirit. Leave this body." She beat her chest and spoke in monotone. Despite this, there was an otherworldly power to her words.

Teacher came to after the dark spirit had been drawn out of the boy. When I asked her the meaning of her words, which spoke of past, present, and future as if they were happening in the present moment, she could only make vague approximations. The words were not her own after all; she was truly possessed by a *kamui*.

I'm sure she could teach me much, but I would never be able to conjure up a spirit that was not my own.

Teacher left to attend to another matter, leaving me alone with the patient.

The boy stirred. He rolled to his side and opened his eyes. He smiled when his eyes met mine. "Have I crossed over?"

"No. You are alive. The men found you in the woods. Your *amip* were drenched. You still have a fever. What happened to you? Why is their blood on your shirt?"

"I don't remember. I don't know how I got here or whose blood that is."

"Well, you should get some rest. We can escort you back home only once you're fully healed," I said, finally letting go of his hand.

"I'm not going back."

"Why not?"

"♫ Because with a snuggle and love. A kiss and a hug. The fox would always guide him home ♫," he said, placing his hand on mine.

Eyes filled with dreams are truly a beautiful sight.

I pulled my hand away. I could feel my cheeks getting flushed. "You should rest. I'll watch over you. But don't talk too much. Save your energy. You're still weak. You haven't fully recovered."

He nodded. "Will you hold my hand?"

"Yes…I can do that. It's good to see you again."

"It's the second time I've visited your village now," he said with a weak smile.

"This isn't the Shitumbe village. It's Moyuk, a village of outcasts. After my *aiai* was killed…I…I did something horrible. I was banished, never to return home. But just like the song says, you can find home anywhere. It goes beyond location and transcends tribe."

"I suppose we're both banished, *chiri-po*," he said, lifting up the blood stained section of his shirt.

"Yep. And were both apprentices now, *isepo*," I said, pulling out my special staff topped with a *niwok*.

"This village really is unlike the others. Hey, *chiri-po*, I suppose I never told you my name."

"Yeah, but I did. It's Ebui. Where did you get *chiri-po* from? I'm a proud fox not a little bird."

"You sang to me and you're little, so you're *chiri-po* now."

"And you are?"

"I was named by my father. I was a meek *aiai*, so it's not a very good name."

"How bad can it be?"

He looked away from me. "Eoha. It means to become empty."

"That's a great name!"

"It is?"

"For a shaman becoming empty is a vital skill. And if you're empty, then that means you have plenty of room in your heart," I said with the biggest smile I could muster.

"It's just as my vision said: you will be rescued by a *shiretok* girl," said Eoha, gazing into me.

Beautiful. Am I really beautiful?

I looked away and covered my flushed cheeks. "*Haphap*. Now, please, be silent. We can chat once you're feeling better."

"One last thing. Do you have a *chikappo*? The shaman of my village always uses one to drive away illness."

"I don't."

"Well, I see no reason the charm has to be a physical object. Can I have a *chopchose* instead?" he asked, puckering his lips.

Teasing me even though he's sick. He'll recover in no time.

"Go to sleep." I leaned over and kissed his forehead.

Eoha smiled at me and closed his eyes.

For four years I stayed at the Moyuk village. Eoha and I trained as apprentices every day. When it came time for possession training, I failed miserably, no matter how hard I tried. Eoha refused to train, if only to not make me feel inferior. Near the end of the third year, I was confident and skilled enough to heal people on my own; we both were. It felt like the curse surrounding me had been lifted. Then one day I received a premonition. It wasn't anything colorful or metaphorical. There wasn't even an image.

It was my teacher's voice. "You've killed me."

That's all it said.

I awoke with cold sweats in my bed.

"Your first vision," said Hechaka, pride beaming from her wrinkled face.

"Yes, I...."

"Congrats!" Eoha picked me up in a heartfelt embrace.

"What was it? No, let me guess. It's about me and about you. *Ainu katu ehange*. The time for me to leave this world is fast approaching," said Teacher in a tone of ease,

"What? No, that's not what it said." I clenched my fists.

"I had the same vision when we first met. I'll admit I was confused at first. I told you our destinies were connected, remember? Ah, this will be a great opportunity for a final lesson." Teacher stared off through the east window.

Final lesson.

I felt dizzy.

Three days passed. I avoided Teacher at every turn. I even left the village on the third day but got lost and ended up back where I had started. It was as if all the *kamui* were conspiring against me.

Could the wrath of that old woman's ghost have been more powerful than I had predicted? Was this my punishment for leaving through the east window? Or was I always a doomed child?

I sat up on a hill overlooking the village.

How long before they are all devoured by my curse?

I gazed up at the stars, searching for answers within their twinkling patterns.

Chapter 3: Bound by the Cosmos

Complete darkness, then dots of light came into being. The one gazing at them wasn't doing so leisurely. The gaze was intense and fully aware. It noticed patterns in the stars. Each *rikop* shined but the light emitting from them felt ominous.

My gaze shifted back to the earthly plane.

The one who had taught me everything I knew looked up at the starlit sky with a smile.

"How can you smile?" I asked, on the brink of tears.

"Why not?" asked Hechaka, still looking into the night sky.

"You're going to die."

"Yes, and the *Kotan Karo Kamui* has been kind enough to let me know when."

I grabbed onto her hand. "Why can't I save you?"

"You'll make a great *tusu-guru*," she said, placing her hand over mine.

"The stars foretell great misfortune in the coming years. I can't help anyone without you."

"I have never done anything. I am merely a vessel."

"You cured my mother. You've saved so many people. I still have so much to learn. You need to teach me more." Tears were already beginning to well up in my eyes.

"You can't run away from your destiny. It will find you, just as death has found me."

"I…I can't do this," I said, pulling my hand away.

46

How can she expect me to kill her?

"You don't have a choice."

"I refuse to!"

"Look up there. We can't escape what's written. Great calamity is creeping upon us. But remember, after every collapse comes a renewal."

"I can't do the ceremony on my own."

"You have Eoha with you as well and the other shamans."

"No. They are depending on you."

"You're here for a reason. You know this must be done. How you plan to do it...that's up to you."

"Why me? You're *onne*; why not let time take you?"

"*Onne?* By that do you mean valued or aged?"

"I meant aged, but of course I value you. You're my teacher."

"You can't convince me otherwise. It's been decided. Hmm, I wonder how you'll do it."

I put my arms around Hechaka's arm and leaned my head against her. "I can't do it." I hugged her tightly. "I love you. You're my teacher. You're even more than that! You're my grandmother! You can't leave until I'm ready. I'm not ready yet, okay?"

"I have taught you much...but your family is still your blood. You must show your true family *uainu*."

"I can never return to them, so why should I bother feeling anything for them. Even if I went back, the villagers wouldn't allow me in. This is my home, and you are my only family now."

"Stay strong. If you don't decide how you're going to end me…soon enough it will happen and not the way you intended. We don't want that, now do we? The more you postpone destiny, the fewer paths you can take."

"I'm only confident as a mystic because of you. I owe you everything. I can only heal people due to your teachings. You gave my life meaning when it had none. I love you dearly!"

"Ah, that will do," said Hechaka, her voice fading.

The arms became limp around me. Her head fell upon my shoulder.

I miss her already.

I stayed in Teacher's limp embrace for a while longer, but eventually I had to stand up. I had to rise to my feet and go back to the village. It was inevitable.

I found my *chisei* in the darkness. Each step I took felt predetermined. I had finally lost my illusion of control. It was as if I had been possessed by a spirit. Each motion was an observation, not an action. I spoke to no one. I had nothing to say anyway. I walked past the sleeping women who shared the cabin with me, careful not to disturb them, and made it to my bed. The night air was cold. I huddled for warmth inside my bear skin blanket. Odd as it may sound, the skin gave me a sense of comfort that no other material could.

It always made me feel like a little bear cub, cuddling against its mother's warm fur.

But the warmth didn't last. Soon it made me feel cold, sad, and alone. I put on three blankets, but the chill would not leave.

Morning came as it always does and always will. Now more than ever I realized the futility of my actions.

I can't stop time. Everyone I know will die, myself included. Such is the fate of mortals.

My eyes opened on their own and before I knew it, I was back on my feet. I rushed over to teacher's *chisei* for early morning lessons. It was only after I entered that it hit me. I fell to my knees.

She was gone.

This must have been how my brother felt. I never knew our blood mother, but he did. He loved her dearly. Even when he smiled at me, his eyes didn't. They always glared. They spoke his thoughts "*You killed her. You took mother away.*"

I felt something on my cheek.

Tears. I was crying.

I wiped my eyes clean but they kept coming.

"Tears are for those who have yet to accept fate." That was what Teacher would say, and it would always make the flow of sadness stop. But now I realized it was her wrinkled smile that calmed me, not the words themselves.

I was on the ground, sobbing. My hands were clinging onto my sacred staff.

I don't deserve this.

If only she knew the truth. I couldn't see spirits. I was never possessed by a *kamui*. The only gift I had was lying. I lied my way into becoming her student. I lied because I thought she could save me, give me power and a purpose that I did not possess. I wanted something to live for. And now I have to keep the lie going until death gives me its mercy.

No. There is one other option.

I packed some food and a few of my belongings and, after properly fastening my *tara*, hoisted them up with my head—which was protected by a cotton cloth. I went back to the hill where Hechaka was resting. After digging a hole and placing my teacher inside, I held up my staff.

"Thank you, chief *kamui*, for bringing me and my teacher together."

"So, she's really gone now," said Eoha as he walked up to me.

Together we wrapped Teacher's body in mats and placed the dirt over the mats. We placed *chi-ehoroka-kep*, special *inao* that were shaved from bottom to top and made many prayers for her well being in the next world.

I turned to Eoha after wiping away my tears.

In the four years we had been together, I had seen him transform from a mischievous boy into a wise, but still at times mischievous, young man. His face was still rounded, as was his nose—both which gave him the look of a baby. He had a slender build and lanky arms that could bend in ways I thought weren't possible. His black hair was cut in the shape of a quarter moon, and he tended to it daily for reasons beyond me. Just like my brother, he had yet to grow any hairs on his chin. His clothes were loose and he only carried a single *chitarape*, which was slung around his right arm, filled with potions, leaves, and other remedies. His amber eyes always lit up whenever they met mine, even though he was in many ways superior to me as a shaman. Though I was a year older than him, I felt that he had wisdom far beyond me.

I stood up and looked into his mystical eyes. "I can't stay here. I'm going back home."

Eoha turned to me and gripped my hand. "Stay with me. Please. There are other mystics here. We can continue our training."

"How long before I have a vision leading to your death? I'm done being a shaman. I'm going back to my village. I'll work in the gardens with my mother. You stay here. Become a powerful *tusu-guru* in my stead." I leaned over and kissed his forehead.

"Let me come along. The forest can be deceptive, especially at night."

"Fine, but only as far as the village outskirts. Pack your things and come right back, okay?"

He nodded and rushed off.

I sat by the unmarked grave. "You deserve better than this. You were beloved in our village. I never should have had you train me. It's only led to misfortune. Maybe, they're right. *Matnep* aren't meant to be *tusu-gurus*." I set my staff at her grave and cried.

"I'm ready."

I turned to see Eoha. I got up, grabbed his hand, and headed back to my village.

On our journey we stopped by a lake. After looking up at the cloudy sky— perhaps pondering about the coming weather—Eoha sat down next to me and dropped some berries into my hands.

"This is your chance," he said with a grin.

"For what?" I asked, licking the berry juice off my finger.

"To see what a beautiful Ainu you are, *chiri-po*," he said, gesturing to the lake.

"Oh no. Mother warned me about reflective surfaces. For each second you spend in front of one, months are sapped away from your life."

"Your brother goes fishing, doesn't he? I'm sure he's seen his reflection a number of times. I don't think you need to worry if it's a *heshi*," he said, splashing his feet in the water.

"I suppose you're right."

I hope I'm not ugly.

I stepped up to the lake and waited for the *aka* to calm. Ever so gradually my visage formed. I was still a bit shorter than Eoha, which he made apparent by placing his hand on my head. There was a sooty, dark blue tattoo mark around my lips.

I remembered that the skin around my lip was cut off in order to make room to place the blue soot in. It was painful and a bit scary, but the colors matched well with the patterns etched on the backs of my hands. Due to my complaining, mother ended prematurely. This left me with a smaller tattoo, and I actually preferred it this way.

My cheekbones were a bit more elevated than I had thought, and my cheeks had a rosy complexion to them. My blue eyes sparkled despite my fatigue. I suppose the color must have been passed down to me by the one my brother calls mother. The blue beads around my neck complemented my facial features. My long brown *attush*, made from the inner bark of elm trees, was held together with shells. The little fox at the hip was a special design I learned from my mother, and I was never told it was inappropriate at the village of outcasts. Around my wrists were bluish bracelets embroidered by my mother. The only thing out of sorts was my hair, though my headdress was lovingly decorated. My mother usually cut and combed it, so it was too long—now down to my elbows—and it was clumped like a bird's nest. Still, I suppose I was pretty.

"See, what did I tell you?" asked Eoha, handing me a blue shell he found at the bottom of the lake.

"*Haphap*. We should get going," I said, fastening the shell to my dress.

"You are most welcome, *chiri-po*. Onward!" he cheered, rushing off ahead of me.

We arrived by morning and slid past some men who were going out on a hunt.

"Eoha, this is as far as you go. Wait here. They might not accept me. And if they don't, then I want to go back with you."

He suddenly embraced me.

He felt so warm.

I kissed his cheek, nodded, and then went back to my village.

Before I made it to my old *chisei*, a hand grabbed my wrist. I was suddenly lifted off the ground and pulled into a hug.

"*Mataki*, you're safe. Father's prayers have been well received."

Brother hated me for killing his mother. He was the one who killed my baby. Despite this, my arms went around his back and returned the affection.

Just seeing a familiar face after all this time was incredible.

My brother was now nineteen, a full-fledged man and fully adorned in *tonto* armor. He was strong, squarely built, thick-chested, and taller than any *ainu* I had seen. He had messy long hair and only a few hairs on his rounded chin that stuck up like *inao* at the *rorun-puyara* altar. A bow and arrow, war club, and some offerings were poking out from the pack slung around his shoulders. His eyes sparkled like a *rikop* pattern of good fortune in the night sky.

Once my feet were back on the ground, his eyes lost their shine.

"I'm sad." I buried my face in his chest.

It reeked of fish.

Dead fish never smelled so good.

"Sadness does us no good. All my tears could not bring her back. Not even my blood could," he said, pulling me off.

"I want to stay here, with my family," I said, trying to hold back my tears.

"Sister. You must leave. Go back to where you came from."

"No! Hechaka, the one who was banished from our village...all because of me...she's dead now."

"She? Your teacher was a man. All *tusu-gurus* are," said my brother.

"You know nothing! Teacher may have had a man's body, but she had a woman's nurturing spirit."

"I'm sorry for your loss. He...she was a great Ainu," said my brother, putting his hand on my shoulder.

I launched myself into him. "Please, let me come with you. I don't want to go back to that place. Everything there reminds me of Hechaka. It forces me to acknowledge her death. I won't go back."

"You must."

"I refuse!"

"A mere two days after you left, someone in the village became very ill. They moved on that very night," said my brother in a whisper.

"And they think it's my fault!"

"It wasn't long before the plague broke out. We've been fighting it for the past four years. Some have lost husbands, others wives, brothers are without sisters, and sisters without brothers. Whole families have been wiped out. There are only half as many of us as there once were. They think the plague is the tangible wrath of the old woman's ghost. They think it's your fault. If you return, I don't think you'll survive three days."

Is it my fault? Did I really cause all that pain, all that death? Teacher was right: there is nothing more terrifying than the wrath of a woman.

"I can't go back there. Please, brother. If you care about me, even a little bit, let me stay," I said, gripping onto his shirt.

"I will talk with the *paunguru*. But it may take time. Go back to your new village. Stay strong, sister. I will find you and bring you back if I can convince the chief."

"Okay. I'll try. Tell father I said hello."

"I will," he said with a smile.

"And give mother a big hug for me," I said with a smile.

"Y-yes. I will tell her you stopped by. Now, hurry, you must leave."

I nodded and turned away from him.

Why can't I be strong like him?

Eoha and I went back to the Moyuk village. Upon returning, he told the other shamans the news of our teacher's passing. That night he held me in his arms until I cried myself to sleep. After a few days, I joined him to continue our training under a different teacher. I was easily distracted and refused outright when the vision training began. I never again wanted to see into the future.

It would only bring misfortune to those around me.

Around twenty days later, when Eoha and I were staying up late chatting by the hill, we heard something rustling in the bushes.

Too big to be a raccoon and too small to be a bear.

It was a man. I raced down the hill and lost my footing. Before Eoha could come to my aid, a familiar rough hand picked me up off the ground.

It belonged to my brother.

"Did they say I can return?" I asked.

"Not exactly," he said, nodding to Eoha to let him know I was in good hands.

"Then what is it?" I asked, pulling at his shirt.

"They sent me here to beg you to return," he said, lowering his head.

"What happened?"

"Our last remaining *tusu-guru*, Eikashu, left this world a few days ago…"

That's what he gets for leading the ceremony to kill my baby.

"…as did father."

All the blood in my body froze. The warmth in the world was gone in an instant.

Father.

"The shaman was taken from us by the plague, but father...he fought bravely against the Horokeu. But in the end, *an-raige*," said my brother, his bottom lip quivering.

Father was killed.

"Who did it? Who took him away from us?"

"There's no way of knowing. But it makes no difference. I swore at his grave that I would kill every last one of them."

My mind shifted back to the Horokeu man who once saved my life, the one who still lived at the Moyuk village. I pictured his face cracked open by my brother's war club. It was refreshing and disturbing all at once.

I put my arm around my brother's.

"Does mother know?"

"Y-yes. I told her. It was the first time I've spoken to Okira's wife in a long time," said my brother, visibly shaken up.

"Did he kill a lot of them? Before...*an-raige*?" I asked, gripping my brother's rough hand.

"Yes. He killed one of their greatest warriors before he succumbed to the *surugu* in their arrows."

"It's *hatto-an* to use poison against another *ainu*, even in warfare."

"The Horokeu have no morals. No doubt the *kamui* they worship are the same dark *kamui* who brought the plague to our village," he said, clenching his free hand into a fist.

"You don't think it's my fault?"

"Please, you're not that powerful and neither was that old woman. This plague is a sign of a shift in power between the *kamui*. The *kunne* is going against the *koshne*, and the dark *kamui* are gaining ground. It's possible that the *nitne kamui* is involved. Of course, I know of no such things, but that is what the *tusu-guru* said when the plague hit him. There will still be those who blame you, but even they know they need you now." He crouched down and wiped a strand of hair away from my face.

The stars told of great misfortune. Could this plague be the omen they showed us?

Eoha came up to us and handed me our teacher's staff.

"Was that in your bag?"

"Teacher told me to give it to you once you accepted her passing. I wanted to pass it on earlier, but I was nervous. You're going to be a full-fledged shaman now. Hechaka would be so proud of you," said Eoha, beaming at me.

I took Teacher's staff from his hands. "Has the village been informed of the shaman's passing?" I asked, shifting toward my brother.

"No. The chief has told everyone that the *tusu-guru* is afflicted with *kamui irushka tashum*. The plan is to inform them once you've returned. You will come back, won't you?"

"Yes. I'll get packed up," I said with a strained smile.

"One last thing. There wasn't time to ask before, but why is there no pattern on your clothes?"

"Oh, that's because this village welcomes people from all tribes. We are a village of outcasts. We no longer belong to any tribe. But I still stitched a little fox," I said, showing him the design on my hip.

"You will always be Shitumbe."

"Of course and they don't ask us to denounce our tribe. It's a really peaceful village. We have our own customs and beliefs. In our village it's okay for women to be—"

"Are there any Horokeu there?" asked my brother, his eyes becoming slanted.

"Of course not. We're welcoming but not crazy."

I hope he believed me.

"You there, boy. What tribe did you belong to?" asked my brother.

Eoha put two fingers on the top of his head. "Isepo. Well, I was one but now I am a Moyuk."

"Isepo are allies, but what are Moyuk? I've never heard of that tribe."

"We are a tribe of outcasts. We are intelligent and crafty scavengers, just like raccoons."

"I suppose that makes sense. Why were you banished?" asked my brother, stepping up to Eoha.

"Enough! He's my closest friend. I won't let you interrogate him. I'm going back to my *chisei* to pack my things, and then I'll meet with you here."

"Understood. Hey, sister…your old clothes…the ones with the Shitumbe pattern, do you still have them?"

"Yes. I've kept them safe," I said with a little smile.

"Good. Put them on. I'll be waiting right here."

Eoha looked up at me. "Will I see you again?"

"Of course you will! At the next inter-tribal meeting. We'll both lead the ceremony," I said with a grin.

And we'll rescue the bear cub too.

"Hey, boy, uh, what's your name?" asked my brother.

"Eoha. And you are?"

"Akno. I'd like to talk to you. You got a moment?"

"Sure."

"Well, go on, *mataki*. We need to head out as soon as we can."

I nodded and headed back to my *chisei*.

After gathering my things, changing into the shirt mother had knit me, and giving a big farewell hug to Eoha, I began my journey back home. Brother and I walked for hours before he finally spoke to me.

"After the plague, like I said, there aren't many of us."

I had almost forgotten.

Was it really my fault?

Brother lifted up his bow and aimed it at a bird on a branch. "We can't get enough to eat with only the men doing the hunting. Would you like me to teach you *emoni*?" he asked, releasing the arrow.

The arrow hit the branch and the bird flew away.

"See? Even experts like myself mess up every once in a while. Want to have a go?" he asked, offering me the bow.

He missed on purpose.

He probably just wants to embarrass me. No, he's going to make me feel like I'm skilled and then show me just how much better he is.

I'll just have to prove him wrong.

"I suppose I could try," I said, grabbing at the bow.

"Uh-uh, not yet. Before every hunt it is important to pray to the fire *kamui*," he said, pulling out a freshly shaved *inao*.

"I'm the *tusu-guru*, so I'll lead, okay?"

"But you don't know what we say," he said, pulling the *inao* out of my reach.

I snatched it and held it between my palms. "Fire *kamui*, divine messenger, I ask that you give us your *inunuke* on the hunt we are about to embark on. May we find plentiful food and return safely." I handed him back the *inao*. "How was that?"

"It's not exact, but you had reverence and that's what counts. So are you ready?"

Oh yeah, I'm ready.

I nodded with a big grin.

After handing me the bow and a few arrows, he got behind me and gripped my arms. "That's it, pull back a bit more. Good. Now getting the proper shot is all about concentration and intention. Aim at the center of the tree."

Concentration and intention—I'm going to do great!

I focused until the feeling of his hands on my arms left, until the tree itself was gone and all there was before me was that single spot. My fingers let go.

The arrow sped through the air and hit just below the target.

"Yes!" I exclaimed with a hop.

"Heheh! Good show. Still it's harder with a moving target," he said, scanning the trees.

"I bet I could take down a deer," I said, loading up another arrow.

"Not yet you can't. You make too much noise when you walk. A deer wouldn't come within range unless it was deaf."

I knew it. This is all just to mock me. I'll show him.

I spotted a squirrel peeking into a hole in the tree.

Ainu of all tribes behold: the very first girl to be a mystic and the very first shaman who can double as a hunter.

I released the arrow.

The squirrel fell off the tree. Though I aimed for the head, I only hit its little back. The squirrel was writhing around and crying.

Crying...just like my little one. My aiai. What have I done?

"Sister, stay focused." Brother fired an arrow through the squirrel's skull. It stopped moving. "You always want to get a sure kill. Ainu aren't the only ones who have souls, all *chikoikip* do, whether land, air, or sea. We also aren't the only creation that can be vengeful. Not that you should worry about a squirrel, but let's say it's a larger animal, like a b—wolf! Well wolves are difficult, but I've taken down a few. Anyways, you don't want them to see your face. That's also why it's best to blind the creature before the kill. And, if you aren't grossed out by the idea," my brother plucked out the squirrel's right eye and popped it in his mouth, "eat the eyes."

My stomach churned.

"That's disgusting."

"Haha. Yeah, I thought you'd say that. But you know, there was a time, before you and I were even born, that mother was infertile. They found out soon after their marriage. It wasn't long before rumors began that one of them had sinned grievously against the *kamui*. She tried many things, visited many *tusu-gurus*, but still she never got pregnant. One day, after a successful hunt, our father came home and served her the heart of an *at kamui*."

"A *kamui*? How do you eat a *kamui's* heart?" I asked, sticking out my tongue.

"No, *at kamui* means the divine prolific one, it is a type of furry bird. Father served her the bird's heart without her knowledge, and a few months later, she got pregnant with me. If it weren't for that animal giving up its *ishu*, I never would have been born," said my brother softly.

"I don't believe it. I think her desire to have a kid finally broke the curse upon her. That's what happened."

"Well, you definitely got the basics of a bow and arrow. Let's move onto traps," he said, beckoning me closer with an open hand.

"So is that all boys know: how to kill and how to pray?" I asked, sticking out a tongue.

"We're taught how to make bows, arrows, traps, and offerings. We're taught how to hunt, fish and read the weather. We learn names of lakes, hills, mountains, tree *kamui* and some of us are even taught how to make poison. So, we know how to pray, kill, and identify landmarks," he said with a grin.

"Well, girls are taught how to cook, make clothes, embroider, make tattoos, garden, cut wood, nurse children, cry at a funeral—which is way more fun than it sounds—and above all we are taught not to disrespect men. So we create art and tools, learn how to properly wail at a funeral, raise children, and make the food. Seems we should be the ones leading the tribe," I said, sticking out my tongue.

And one day we will.

"I think the wise should lead, not the ones who work the hardest," said my brother.

"So, were you taught how to make poison?" I asked, squinting at the arrow tips.

"Yes, but that's very advanced and it's dangerous. Let's stick with traps for now, okay?"

I nodded and smiled. "Okay."

On the way back home, my brother taught me how to make *akbe*, a type of spring bow for hunting deer and *akbe-imok*, a spring trap used to catch raccoons, otters, and other small animals.

"Wait, but what if a fox gets caught in it?" I asked.

Brother tossed a rock in the trap. The rock was gripped by the string. "Well then the fox gets hoisted up into the air and we get to eat," he said, flicking the suspended stone.

"But we're Shitumbe!"

"Yes, foxes are our tribal symbol, but they aren't our guardian deity. You've eaten fox before."

"What? I didn't know. I just thought meat was…well, meat," I said, shuffling my feet. "I'm never eating *shumaune* again!"

"Does that mean you don't want any squirrel?" asked my brother, handing me thin slices of flesh.

That was once part of a living being.

"Are you kidding? I was the one who shot him. He'll come back and haunt me. Why take the risk? I'm done eating meat. Never, ever, ever again am I going to put something that once had a soul in my mouth."

"Then why did I waste my time teaching you how to hunt?" he asked, air puffing out from his nostrils.

"It's all you know and I…I just wanted to be with you," I said.

I can't even remember the last time we bonded.

"What about *chep*? Will you eat *chep*? Do you want to learn how to *emoni*?"

"Fish aren't vegetables. They have a soul too. Last thing I want is them circling around me in my dreams. Let's just head back, okay?"

"Fine. But in case you get lost, I'll show you what plants not to eat," he said, tossing me a mushroom.

"Ooh. Nice find. Did you know if you mix this in with soup it can cure fatigue?"

"Can't say I did. That's good to know."

"Yep, looks like I'll be the one teaching you," I said with a grin.

"I suppose so. Teach me as we move along. We should be able to make it back by nightfall if we pace ourselves."

We arrived at our village the next morning. Everyone was outside of their tents and seated for the early meal. The gatherers had found plentiful amounts of *ratashkep*.

I'm hungry.

"First we must tell the *paunguru* you've returned. Come with me. I'm not letting you out of my sight," he said, leading me past the crowd.

We arrived at the chief's *chisei*, which was a bit bigger than the others. In the Moyuk village, all the homes were the same size and rather than one chief and two sub-chiefs, we had three chiefs of equal status and power.

Brother approached the door, cleared his throat and entered.

He sat cross-legged at the hearth near the chief. They rubbed their hands together for a while.

It was the customary greeting for *ainu*. In the village of outcasts, both men and women initiated any conversation by performing the greeting before we entered someone's *chisei*.

The *paunguru* and my brother went back and forth, wishing *inunuke* upon each other, their families, relatives, etc. They ended the ritualistic greeting by stroking their beards, or in my brother's case—the few hairs on his chin, all the while talking about the matter at hand.

It was only after they stopped stroking their chins that I was invited to speak.

It's been so long. Hope I remember everything.

I removed my headdress and placed it over my arm. I brushed the front locks of my hair to the side and placed my hand over my mouth.

Teacher was right. Even with something as simple as a greeting, women are made to know they are inferior.

After getting an invitation to speak, I cleared my throat and pulled my hand away. "Thank you for allowing me to return."

I knew not what else to say.

Brother cleared his throat, wished blessings on the chief, and walked out.

I did the same but had to walk backward out of the cabin. After all, it was taboo for a woman to show her back to a man.

Wait. This is just another way to keep us women suppressed. These little things are all thin ropes, fastening themselves to our psyche. They keep us bound, just like a scared little bear before it is ridiculed and sacrificed.

I began to tear up.

Brother grabbed my hand and walked me to our *chisei*. "You must miss mother."

"Oh I can't wait to see her. We have a lot to catch up on. And father too! I missed them both so much!"

Brother shifted his gaze to the ground. "I told you, father is…."

Dead. That's right, he was killed by the Horokeu. It doesn't seem real.

"I have to prepare for the funeral. I'll pick you up when it's time. Don't go outside. It isn't safe for you here yet, understood?"

I nodded.

Brother guided me past the chief's *chisei*, which was only a bit larger than the other homes. Before long we arrived.

Home.

It looked the same as ever: walls made of reeds fastened together by the inner bark of elm wood, the porch by the west end where I would often gaze at the stars with mother, the south end exit where father would go to get extra fire wood, screens made of reeds, the *rorun-puyara* where my father and brother would sit at daily for prayer, and situated on eight stilts around a small plot of land where mother and I gardened.

It was nostalgic.

"I don't ever want to leave again," I said, latching onto his arm.

"You won't have to. The house is under my custody now, and I would never give it up. Welcome home, *mataki*," said my brother, opening our door.

In the center was the *hoka*, currently unlit. This was the vessel where the fire *kamui* gave enough warmth to save mother's life but not enough to save the mother before her.

Mother was seated on an *aputki* in her corner, knitting our pattern into a garment. Her brown eyes met mine and the needle dropped.

It happened so fast. I wasn't sure if her arms coiled around me first or if mine grabbed onto her before them. Either way, she was warm.

Alive and warm.

She looked so beautiful. Her forehead and arms were decorated with beautiful patterns—something I wouldn't experience because I would never marry. A beaded necklace, earrings, rings, and bracelets all came together to make her inward beauty project to all who saw her. It took me a moment to realize she was wearing a widow's bonnet, and her head was completely shaved. This was when it really sunk in.

Father was gone.

I cried in her arms till my eyes were sore.

She made me up my favorite stew with peas, along with some beans and potatoes. It looked so vital, and it never had dead animals in it anyway. I picked up the cup and sat in mother's lap.

"O, chief *kamui*, our nourisher, I thank thee for this food: bless it to the service of my body," I said before bringing the soup cup to my lips.

It tastes like home.

Having finished my soup, I started cleaning my cup with my index finger. Mother suddenly asked me to tell her about my journey.

I set down my cup, grabbed her shoulders, and wept.

I lost track of time telling her all about the Moyuk village, about my teacher, about the apprentice boy, and about all the things I learned. Most of all we talked about father, our fondest memories, his achievements, and how much we will miss him. Soon after the sun went away, my brother came in.

"It's time. We'll need a *tusu-guru* to conduct the service," he said, leaning against the door.

I walked with him into the crowd. Everyone stared at me as I approached. I noticed many of the women had shaved their heads, likely hiding the resulting scars beneath their mourning bonnets. Some of the men had cut their hair short, a few had even torn out not only their hair but most of their beard as a testament to how much the loss of their wives meant to them.

So much pain and I'm the cause, aren't I?

Brother grabbed my hand. "Stay strong. They don't know yet but soon they'll be grateful you're here."

Strong, okira, just like father. I never realized how similar they are. Brother and father have the same fortitude.

The elder patted the ground next to him.

I sat down next to the *paunguru* of my village.

I looked at his wrinkled face.

How long before my curse claims his life as well?

He looked into my eyes and nodded ever so slightly. He raised his hand, immediately calling everyone's attention to him. "Eikashui has moved on." He grabbed my arm and raised it. "Ebuike is our *tusu-guru* now."

Flower? Well, I suppose I'm no longer a bud anymore.

I gripped my teacher's staff.

Banished, trained in a village of outcasts, and journeyed back home. So many things have happened. But here I am now, serving the shaman for my people.

Silence befell the crowd.

Ainu were taught to respect our elders and the *paunguru* in particular. Still, I doubt even the chief could placate them now.

They wanted me dead.

My brother was the first to raise his hand, though out of respect for the chief, not for me. The other's followed, but their gestures were empty.

Everything feels empty.

The mystic's funeral was one of the happiest I had been to. As always, the commoners were in the back and there was ample rice wine, which was also known as *tonoto*—the official milk. I didn't mind funerals. It was the day after that would always bother me. Most of the men would reek of *arakke* and go around in a stupor.

I had to hold in my laughter when my brother drank with the other men. As always, he would use a moustache lifter—a long and thin device used to keep the mustache from going in the rice wine—even though he only had a few hairs growing.

Thankfully both my brother and my father always drank in moderation and only did so during a celebration, never out of mourning or for leisure. Father was aware that drinking caused more problems than it solved, and my brother decided to follow father's example. Hopefully, there wouldn't be too much drinking at this ceremony. The man who moved on was already very old. Now that I was going to take up the mantle, our people wouldn't be without their mystic. Still, some glared at me between sips.

"Proceed," said the chief, looking at me.

I stared at him blankly.

Am I supposed to conduct the ceremony…right now?

My brother tapped my shoulder. "You'll do fine."

I took a deep breath.

Okay. It's time. Time to find out what destiny has in store for us.

I walked to the center of the group and arranged the sticks in the proper order. I had to make sure the central stick was facing east. I created a circle around the pile with the final stick, before tossing it in with the others.

I closed my eyes. I chanted as I knocked the ignition sticks together.

A flame came into being.

So far, so good.

With great care I leaned over the batch of sticks and set them aflame.

The heat bit my hand, reminding me that I was only a mediator for its message.

In the sky something whizzed by. It was a broom star and bore special meaning to mystics. War, famine, flood, I knew not what it meant, but I knew that a great calamity was on approach.

But the misfortune in the stars should already be over. My people suffered a plague. What else could befall us? I felt dizzy.

I saw my brother looking up at me.

I have to stay strong.

I took a deep breath and continued the ritual. I let the fire cook for a bit—placing my awareness on it and further away from the scornful gaze of the people around me.

I could jump in right now. Sure it would be painful, but it's what they all want. It's probably what's best for the tribe. No. I'm being selfish. Teacher left me with a mission. I have to prove that a woman, or even a girl, can be a proper tusu-guru. I have to do this right, if only for her.

The fumes entered my nostrils. I centered my thoughts to shift my awareness.

Fire everywhere. Bodies…so many bodies.

Is this the future?

The blood from the bodies crawled toward me.

This is a nightmare.

I came to my senses, looking at my brother.

"What did you see?" he asked.

Strange. His eyes didn't look at me with disdain. They looked at me with worry, maybe even care. My birth killed his mother. Why is he looking at me like this?

"Sister, you must tell us what you saw."

I now noticed my hands were shaking. No, not only my hands—my whole body was trembling like a raging river.

I may have been incapable of seeing spirits, but I had a knack for divination. Why did my only talent bring me such misfortune?

"Tell us exactly what you saw," said the chief, his eyes fixated on me.

"I…there was…a fire. It consumed the cabins. There were many dead."

"How many?" asked my brother.

"I don't know. There were *kaisei* as far as the eye could see. And blood…it was everywhere."

"You trust this child?" asked a voice from the crowd.

My brother turned his head but was unable to locate the voice's point of origination. "Ebuike is not a child. My sister has been through fourteen cycles. If not for Eikashu's passing, she would be searching for a partner for which to wed in two years."

Why was he defending me?

"Trust what you want. I am only speaking what I saw," I said with wisdom far beyond my years.

"How soon before the vision becomes the present?" asked the chief.

"I don't…"

Yes I do.

"The trees will be taller than the cabins. A few years it seems," I said.

"We must be prepared for anything," said my brother, gripping his spear.

"Do you think it is the Horokeu clan?" asked the elder.

"It must be. Who else would attack our village?" asked my brother.

I tapped my brother's shoulder. "I never said there was an attack."

"You said there was blood. Fire does not make blood, *ainu* do. You are right that it may not be the Horokeu clan. In your vision, do you remember seeing any attackers?"

"No, only bodies. Wait, arrows...yes. There was a bamboo-tipped arrow in the neck of one of the bodies, a few more in the area around it. The Horokeu clan use clubs, spears, and stone-tipped arrows in warfare, like we do. We can't say for certain it was them."

The chief's face became pale. "Are you sure that's what you saw?"

"It happened so fast, but that's what I remember," I said.

"Fast? The fire had gone out before you awoke," said my brother.

"I saw an arrow with a bamboo tip. It seems so familiar," I said.

"Isepo," said the chief. "But they are our allies."

This is crazy. Why would Eoha's people attack us?

"We can't be certain of anything. They became our allies out of fear, not kinship. Our ancestors have fought them before," said my brother.

"Careful. We must not incite a battle," said the chief.

"Of course not. I'll take a few men and we'll scope out the area. But we should keep in mind they might not even be preparing to attack yet. It's difficult to place the exact time of the vision. Thank you, *mataki*."

"For what?" I asked, looking up at him.

"For saving us," he said, his smile genuine and beaming.

Saving us.

Brother seized my head and ran his hand down the length of my hair from my crown to my shoulders.

This gesture lit up my spirit. Yet at the same time, it calmed me, reminding me of all the times father used to praise me.

I wasn't alone. Brother believes in me. He truly does.

"When are you leaving?" I asked, my hand gripping his arm without me noticing.

"Soon. You should rest. Head back to our *chisei*," he said, pulling away. Before I knew it, he was gone from my sight.

I got up and searched the crowd for my brother.

He tells me to stay by his side and then he leaves.

I stepped to the side, covered my mouth, and kept my gaze fixed on the ground, as was customary for women to do when men were crossing.

One of the young men bumped into me.

He pushed me away. "Don't you touch me. Your curse already took my sister away." His gaze pierced past my flesh and wounded my spirit.

"Wait, Hapuru, she is dead?" I asked, a cold chill suddenly coming over me.

That can't be true. She was always so healthy and happy. Someone like that couldn't be gone.

"She fell ill the night after you were banished."

"I never meant to hurt her. She was my friend."

Who else has been taken by my curse?

75

"Stay away. All you touch falls to ruin, cursed child," he said as he walked off.

A full-grown man looked at me and spat in my face, one hand raised in a fist, the other holding onto the wrist of his wife. "Murderer. If you take more of my wives from me, I'll kill you myself." He then pulled her along.

What if the plague really was my fault? She is dead because of me.

My eyes watered up.

Where is my brother?

After navigating through the hateful stares of my people, I found my brother.

"You look shaken up. Were you crying? Was it another vision?" he asked, handing one of the men a freshly sharpened arrow.

"I need to talk to you," I said.

My brother signaled the man to leave us.

I looked up at him and I froze up.

"Well, speak."

"Why are you being like this? You've been acting different ever since you went to fetch me from the village of outcasts. Is it because I'm the only shaman the village has now? Is that why you give me *uainu*?"

Brother looked at me with wet eyes. "I've always respected you."

Liar!

"That isn't true. You hated me. You put me outside in the cold mere days after I was born. I heard it from father. You blamed me for mother's death."

The plague, her death, Teacher, father—did all these horrible things happen because of me?

"I was so foolish back then. *Mataki*, can you forgive me?"

"Huh? What? What about you? Can you forgive me for mom's death?"

"I can't. But that's due to my own weakness. You inspire me, *mataki*. I can't just accept how powerless we all are. If I did, I wouldn't be able to fight, to kill those who threaten us. You can do what none of us can. You can enter the darkness and bring light to us."

Was it all in my head? He doesn't hate me? He looks up to me? What's going on?

"You've saved us all. I can't thank you enough."

As my mind tried to make sense of it all, he drifted further and further away.

It was my own projection. The look I saw in his eyes was my own guilt, not his hate.

I nearly fell to the ground.

He was right. I needed rest.

"I'll head back home, okay?"

"No. Stay away from our *chisei*. I'm going to go check it out with some of the other men. Is there a safe place you can stay?"

"Well there's the cave where I was taught. But I don't think you have to—"

"It may not be safe there. Do you know a place that nobody else knows about?"

What was he so worried about?

"Yes. I do."

"Good. Stay there. You can return in the morning. Understood?"

"Am I in danger?" I asked, grabbing his hand.

"I don't know. It's just a precaution. Stay safe, *mataki*."

If he believes in me, then I'll trust him too.

"*Popke no okai un*," I said, with a nod.

"Yes. *Popke no okai un*."

His fingers let go of my hand, and I went into the forest.

Soon enough I found myself deep in the forest in front of a cave.

This was where Hechaka had always entered to find deeper truths. She warned me of its dangers, but now I am ready to face them.

I entered the cave and sat on the rocky ground.

A strong scent overcame me. It was noxious, but my nose welcomed it in as a guest.

It wasn't long before I had another vision.

My brother was naked. His face was pale. Blood dripped from his lips. He was shivering. There was a wound in his chest, a deep wound. The weapon was blurred, but the hand holding it was crystal clear—as was the blood on it. I recognized the bracelet on the hand's wrist. It was my own.

Chapter 4: Eternally Cursed

How can this be happening? I was going to kill him. Why? Nothing makes sense anymore. Think of what Teacher said, "If I don't understand the vision, it can bring about great misfortune." That's right. She died because I gave her the peace of mind necessary to move on. Things are never as simple as they seem. No force on this planet could make me kill my own brother willingly, especially not now. It's probably more of a nightmare anyway. Then again, my dreams and nightmares have all ended up as realities. Let's say it's true…that I do kill him. Why would that be?"

"I knew I'd find you here," said a young, happy voice.

I awoke out of my trance and opened my eyes, slowly re-familiarizing myself with my surroundings.

It was Eoha, my fellow shaman in training. I suppose we aren't equals anymore.

I hope that doesn't change our relationship too much.

"What are you doing here? Has something happened at your village?"

"I came to see you. Things aren't the same without you there," he said with a warm smile.

I stood up. "You want me to try to convince my *paunguru* to let you in the village. I don't have that kind of power. And right now, tensions are very high, even amongst allies."

If I tell him more, that will only make things worse.

"I wouldn't ask you to. What I want is something different, *chiri-po*," he said, gently putting my hand between his.

I looked into his eyes and then turned away.

He was love-stricken. I mean, he's liked me for a long time. I always found it endearing, but what if it's more than that?

"Please, hear me out," he said, his eyes beaming at me.

Did destiny connect him to me? Does he have a role to fulfill for our clan? For what reason have our fates been intertwined?

"You are my dear friend, but you will never be anything other than that," I said, pulling away from him.

"Life isn't the same without you beside me," he said, taking a step closer.

I have to stop this now.

"Okikurumi, the great hero, nearly died from the despair of love. You should learn from his example. You are a powerful shaman. Why can't you just be content with that?"

"Remember that even with the world beneath him and the stars around him, the *chup orosh guru* is lonely. I'd rather die from despair than live with loneliness," he said, putting his arms around me.

"Let go of me!" I yelled, pushing him to the ground.

I won't let my curse take him away. I won't lose him too!

Eoha stood up and approached me. "We don't have to have children, but still," he took something out from his pack and placed it around my neck "I want you to marry me."

He really does think I'm pretty.

"Wait. I can't."

"Why not?"

This is only getting worse! What do I do?

"It isn't common to marry outside your village. I've never heard of an *uiritak* wedding from this village," I said with a shaky voice.

"My father is a Shitumbe and just because it's uncommon doesn't mean it's *hatto-an*. This is the only way I'll be welcomed to stay in your *chisei*. We've lived together for so long. I've wanted to ask for you to marry me for a while now."

He said it again.

"I just could never build up the courage to propose. But now I don't have a choice. If marriage is our only means of continuing to share the same home, then I must marry you."

Why must he be so cute and kind?

"But what about my parents? I mean, my mother, um, my brother would never approve."

"I spoke with your brother before. He gave more than his *inunuke*. He told me to marry you and keep you happy. He only asked one thing in return," said Eoha with an embarrassed smile.

Why must destiny be so intrusive in my life?

"What did he want?"

"Sorry, he asked me not to tell you unless we did marry."

"Well, what about your parents? You would need your parents' approval too."

"It's the children who get the final word. Not even if the parents on both sides will a marriage to be can they force it upon their children."

"Yes, but without their consent we would have to get our own *chisei* and there would be no ceremony."

81

Yes. That's it. I'll say whatever it takes. I have to get this idea out of his head before we're both doomed.

"The ceremony isn't important. What matters is that we're together. Don't you trust me?" His gorgeous amber eyes glistened.

"Of course I do. We switched clothing that one time, remember?"

"Yes. I remember. I suppose considering the dangerous hexes one can place on another through the possession of their *amip*, their truly is no act more trusting. Now that you mention it, it's not uncommon for the betrothed to exchange clothes and live together in their future spouse's *chisei*. I'd like live in your *chisei*," he said, reaching for my hand.

I wanted to pull away, but before I knew it my hand was gripping his. The next moment we were in a warm embrace.

"But I'm cursed. Surely our marriage would only end in disaster," I said, while pressed up against him.

"The necklace I gave you is an *aumshup*. It's the only thing I have to remember my father by. Not only that. It is also a powerful *inao-kike*. It will protect you."

"But who will protect you?"

"I can defend myself. So, will you marry me?"

All the exits are being closed off. Every route is converging at one point. What can I say to stop this?

"You're in such a rush. And remember what happened to the impatient Pen'ambe."

"Yes, but he was a fox and I am a rabbit."

A handsome rabbit.

"True, but I…well, I'm only fourteen!"

Yes, of course! I'm too young to marry. Why didn't I think of that earlier?

"I'm only fifteen," he said with a grin. "But I want something to look forward to when I become a man."

Two years from now. Is that when it will happen, the prophesized end of my people?

"I…I.…"

"We may be diviners, but it's alright if we make our own future every so often. A promise to marry is like a prophecy in itself. Only a matter of time before it's fulfilled," he said, giving me a kiss on the cheek.

Hapuru. His kiss was so soft, yet I feel such a strong warmth.

"I…I'll think it over."

"Thanks, that's all I ask of you," he said with a nod.

I only hope it isn't too late.

"May I have some time alone? I just need to calm my thoughts. I've been under so much stress lately," I said, sitting down.

"And I'm here to help you bear it," he said, leaning his head against my shoulder.

So sweet!

"Please, Eoha. Just for tonight."

He stood up. "Of course. I'll leave you be, *chiri-po. Popke no okai un.*"

"May you be kept warm too," I said with a smile.

He left the cave with steps of hesitation.

The annihilation of my people, potential death of my brother, and now marriage—it was all too much to comprehend. What if they were each stepping stones to one another? Which comes first? What do I do?

I held my teacher's staff to my chest. "Please, give me the strength and the vision to see past all this. How can I save my people?"

I sat in silence and time whisked by.

A hand broke me out of my trance.

"Do you know what's going on?" asked Eoha, pulling me to my feet.

"What do you mean?" I asked, only half aware.

The sun was shining through the vines.

I was more tired than I had thought.

"Six men, your brother leading them, they were listening in on a meeting from my old tribe. Next thing I know they take the chief hostage. Please, you have to talk some sense into him. He'll listen to you, right?" asked Eoha.

"He wouldn't do that without a reason. What was said in the meeting?"

"How am I supposed to know? I was lucky I wasn't spotted. Returning from banishment warrants severe punishment," he said, taking a step back.

"What can I do?"

"I need you to ask your brother what happened. If you don't talk to him, things will only get worse. One of my old friends has rounded up a party to save the *paunguru*. Of course they don't want to hurt your brother, but things could escalate."

He's right. No wait, that's not true. If I'm the one who hurts my brother, then that means as long as I stay away from him, no harm will come to him…at least nothing fatal.

"Intervening would only make things worse."

"You won't try to reason with him?"

"He knows what he's doing. I have faith in him. But take me to see the rescue group. I'll talk to them."

I won't just sit here and do nothing.

"I'm not even supposed to know about them. I can't take you there."

"You will. I know you will," I said, giving him a kiss on the lips.

Soft and warm.

"That's the first time you've kissed me there," he said, gently touching his bottom lip.

"Let's get going," I said, flashing him an extra sweet smile.

"Yuh-yeah. It's not too far from here. I'll lead the way," he said, stepping out in front of me.

I can't live up to his expectations, but that doesn't mean he can't bend to mine a bit. His bond with me can help bring peace to both our tribes.

Eoha was right; in less time than it took for me to unjumble my thoughts, we had made it to the group. They were each carrying spears and a quiver of arrows…all except for one. He was holding a war club.

What was a Horokeu warrior doing with the Isepo clan? Did the Isepo get spears from the Horokeu? Nothing makes sense anymore.

"She means you no harm. She only wants to talk," said Eoha.

I tried to pretend I didn't notice the club. Good thing I was skilled at lying.

"I know my brother well. He will return the chief before the night is up."

"I agree," said the *Horokeu* warrior.

"Good."

"Bring her with us. Now we have bargaining power," he said.

"Hey, wait a minute. You don't have to go that far. I know her brother too. He only attacks when provoked," said Eoha.

"He has our chief hostage. Having a hostage of our own puts us on even ground. The more even we are, the more likely this will not end in bloodshed," said the youngest of the Isepo soldiers.

"And what if he refuses to hand over the *paunguru*? Then what?" asked Eoha.

"We will make him hand over our chief, no matter the cost," said the leader of the specialized squad.

My ankle turned as I made a sprint for safety. Before I knew it, I was on the ground with a spear held to my neck.

Things are escalating so quickly. No matter what, I mustn't see my brother.

"Get away from her!" yelled Eoha before he was slugged by the Horokeu warrior. He fell down flat on his back.

86

"Don't hurt him. I'll cooperate."

Nobody else will suffer because of me.

"Bring her along. I still have his trail," said one of the Isepo warriors.

"Run when you get the chance. I will protect you, *chiri-po*." Eoha bit his thumb and made marks under his eyes and cheeks. He took out a special potion from his arm bag and drank it. He rose up slowly, almost like a marionette.

"Eoha, why make this difficult? Do you value this Shitumbe over your old tribe, more than our chief?" asked an Isepo warrior, his spear at the ready.

Eoha's eyes were vacant. He rushed up to the warrior and slashed his face.

Were his nails always that long and sharp?

I grabbed the spear in front of me and pushed it away. The warrior slammed his foot on my belly and repositioned the spear. I could feel its tip poke a hole in my skin. I turned my attention back to Eoha. His shirt was partially cut, and there was a trail of blood at his chest.

"Stop!" I yelled.

Eoha's fingernails rode up his attacker's arm, carving it up. He then jabbed his hand into the warrior's neck.

Did Eoha just kill someone? No, that wasn't him. Unlike me, he had a connection to the kamui. He was channeling a kamui's essence and a strong one at that. This all seemed so surreal.

The other Isepo warriors made a circle around him. The Horokeu warrior gained ground by a nearby hill. He was aiming his spear.

Oh no.

"Wait! I'll come with you, okay? Don't kill him!"

It was too late. The spear had already been thrown.

It stopped as soon as it hit its intended point.

Simply following its path, like all of us, I suppose. Wait!

The spear was clenched in Eoha's hand. The feat was even more spectacular considering his head was dangling and thus only able to see the ground.

This display of otherworldly power was enough to scare the others off. They picked me up and ran as fast as they could.

"Eoha is a mystic, right? How can he be so skilled in combat? You knew him, right? Tell me," said one of the warriors, keeping his blade at my throat.

"I've never seen him like that. I heard he could channel *kamui*, but I thought they needed a ritualistic space to operate. I thought he was framed for the murder of Shirara, but what if he really did kill him? We need to keep our distance. Do you think he's still following us?" asked the youngest warrior.

Murder. That's why he was banished.

"Doubt it," said one of the warriors before collapsing.

The spear from before had found a new home at the tip of his spine.

Is this another vision? Am I still in that cave? This can't be real?

The youngest warrior was already at his ally's side. "Can you hear me?" he asked, his voice barely coming out.

"He's dead. We better move or we'll share his fate," said the eldest warrior.

Five other men met up with the group, all wielding spears.

More Horokeu?

"The Isepo's banished prodigy killed one of his own. Be careful when you approach him. We'll meet up with you once their *paunguru* has been recovered," said the Horokeu warrior.

The other's nodded and made their way down the hill.

"Eoha!"

I was shouting, screaming for him. But in the end, what was the point? My love for my dear friend isn't enough to keep him from death. But as long as he channeled a *kamui*, a spirit which has transcended destiny, he should be safe from harm.

By the time I turned my attention to the front, I saw him, my brother, and five other men all holding spears up to the Isepo *paunguru*.

I heard all about the Isepo chief from Eoha. He was a bit too idealistic, but I never thought he would harm anyone. Yet his own people had sided with the Horokeu to retrieve him.

The spear fell from my brother's hand once he saw me.

"Tell your men to release the *paunguru*. Now," said the Isepo captain.

My brother's mouth opened, but no words came out.

His fellow warriors turned to him for guidance.

My brother picked up his spear and raised it. "You really have sided with the Horokeu. To think I once called you my brothers," he said, tears finding their way out of his fiery eyes.

"You bring dishonor to all your ancestors by taking our *paunguru*. *Aiona kamui* is watching you, *furep*," said the Isepo captain.

"You worship your chief as if he was the chief *kamui*. Idolatry is against the word of our great ancestor," said my brother.

"Stop! We don't want any more violence. We will trade our chief for your sister. Is that understood?" asked the youngest Isepo warrior.

"A *paunguru* for a *tusu-guru*, that hardly seems fair," said my brother, signaling the others to press their spears closer to the chief.

"We will kill your sister if you don't cooperate!" yelled the Isepo captain.

"A rabbit baring its teeth at a fox. Laughable," said my brother, though I noticed his hands were shaking.

"Cut her," said the leader.

"For every cut you put on her, your chief loses a limb," said my brother, his rage boiling.

"Everyone, calm down!" yelled the youngest warrior. "I just saw my old friend, a dear friend, kill my closest friend. I don't want to see any more death. Please. Let's settle this without bloodshed and go home."

All I want is to go home with my brother.

"The Horokeu clan murdered our people. They killed my father! They killed our *tusu-guru*!" yelled my brother.

"And you've killed many of us, Shitumbe," said the Horokeu warrior.

"Brother. You said the shaman moved on due to sickness. Nobody killed him. If anything, I am responsible," I said in a whisper.

"*Surugu*. He was poisoned," he said softly.

"What. You can't know for certain," I said.

"It was at the Isepo clan's bear ceremony. No feuding allowed and they all drink rice wine. A day later, our shaman falls ill and leaves this world that very night. That's too convenient for a coincidence. And our father was poisoned too. Not by drink but by an arrow! I'll kill every Horokeu and all who call them friend!"

Yet another calamity follows the ceremony.

"What if you're wrong?" I asked.

"I don't need to prove it. A Horokeu spy told us everything. That is before we cut him open."

"Why would they target him? It makes no sense."

Please calm down, my brother.

"The *tusu-guru* is even more important than the *paunguru* in some ways. They heal the sick, mend wounds both physical and spiritual. It is with their power that the *kamui* are channeled and reasoned with. You were their next target. Before I even left with the group, I found two Horokeu warriors outside our *chisei*. With you dead, we would have no shaman to lead our ceremonies," he said, gritting his teeth.

"You know how important she is, both to you and your village. Now let the chief go," said the youngest Isepo warrior.

"Your *paunguru* made secret unions with the enemy, seeking peace with those murders. I took up the spear so that I could usher justice for my people. To allow him to live would be to betray all I believe," he said.

"Would you rather have your sister's death on your conscience? If you need to shed blood, take mine. Let the chief go," said the youngest warrior, breaking down into tears.

"No. Release her now or your *paunguru* loses a limb!" yelled my brother.

"I'll call your bluff. Foxes are tricky creatures, after all. We won't give up our only advantage," said the Isepo warrior leader.

A slice. An arm fell to the ground.

Did he just...?

"Chief!"

All the Isepo warriors rushed at my brother.

The spears turned away from the chief and toward the attackers.

Weapons clashing, blood, and muffled screams. It all felt like another vision.

My brother is safe. If destiny decided I will kill him, then that makes him invincible.

The Isepo warriors fell. I suppose their emotions left them open to attack.

I felt something cut into my side. It was sharp. It hurt.

An arrow had pierced me. The Shitumbe warriors charged at the Horokeu man who had stabbed me.

Was I going to die? No. Impossible. My vision said I was alive. It couldn't have been false. It never is!

The five Shitumbe warriors checked me for wounds.

Wait...only five? Brother!

My brother was on the ground, for the first time looking helpless. A spear was in his chest. The wound was deep.

Before I knew it I was at his side, hands gripping the spear.

Was this the vision? No. He was naked. He is still partially clothed. But here I am, holding the weapon lodged in his chest.

Brother looked up and smiled at me.

I knew it. He won't go down from only one spear.

My brother looked past me and at the men. "Kill him. Kill the Isepo *paunguru*. He couldn't have gone far."

The Shitumbe warriors bowed and then rushed off.

"Let me tend to your wounds," I said.

I lifted up his shirt and placed the salve on his wound. Other than the giant gash, he had no new scars.

"*Mataki*, can you promise me something?" he asked with a smile.

"What?" I asked, carefully cleaning the wound.

"Don't blame yourself. I die a warrior. It isn't your fault. You've saved us. You uncovered the secret alliance," he said, his eyes slowly closing.

"No! You are not dying!" I yelled, griping the spear and slowly pulling it out.

It was deeper than I thought.

The spear had pierced through his flesh. It had pierced into his heart.

I grabbed my head. "No. No. No. I shouldn't have come. I shouldn't have," I said, breaking down into tears.

"That's right. You got captured. You need to be more careful. Promise me you'll be more careful," he said, rising up to look me in the eye.

"I'll be more careful. You can't die, right? You have to kill the traitors. You need to usher in justice in this empty world," I said, gripping his hand tightly.

Please, don't go.

"You have to convince the *paunguru* for me. I can't rest without knowing that every last treacherous Isepo is dead. Tell him what I told you."

"This is because I had the vision. You went out into harm's way because of me."

"I'm a soldier. It's...*ay-oh*...my *ishu*. It's been a great life. Sister, I'm starting to fade. I don't know if anyone's told you this, but you're very beautiful. When you're focused during a trance, you give off the presence of a benevolent *kamui*. You truly have blossomed, *mataki*."

His hand went limp. His eyes closed. That was his last smile.

Brother.

The world no longer felt empty. It was dark. Ominous. It had a *kuroro* of its own. Destiny was conniving and malicious. There was no way to fight it. Worst of all it had chosen me as its target.

I looked up at the night sky.

The twinkling stars weren't showing their beauty. They weren't even sending a message. They were showing off their power. They were looking down at us mortals and deciding how next to make us suffer.

PART 2:

GAMBLING WITH THE GODS

Chapter 5: Fear & Duty

There I was, looking up at the stars, the merciless upper echelon *kamui* did nothing to comfort me. The *kamui* were all worthless. No amount of prayer or *inao* could do anything to amend the situation.

Brother.

His warm hand was still in my grip, but it was an empty warmth…soon to fade like everything else.

I had misinterpreted the prophecy. It appeared like I would be the one to kill him, making him invincible to all others. The vision was showing me removing a spear, not plunging it in.

Of course it was. Why didn't I realize it in time?

My tears were still flowing despite all my efforts to stay *okira*.

May my brother find my father in the next world.

The sadness sapped at my resolve. I didn't want to do anything. Despite the urgent information that only I could pass to the chief, despite my brother entrusting me to do so…I couldn't move. It wasn't that I wanted to die or stay there…holding his hand. All motivation was gone. I merely existed and nothing more.

When I was shaken to my senses, the stars were still in the sky so it couldn't have been too long. My eyes put forth the effort to focus on the object before me.

Isepo? Come to finish the—Eoha!

Still unable to speak, I flung myself on top of him with a sudden burst of energy. Even if I was only hallucinating, I would savor every moment before I would wake up. He had blood on him.

That's right. He was possessed. He killed them...his own people...to keep me safe.

I noticed his smile and smiled back. His hand went over mine and slowly tore me away from my brother.

Goodbye, dear brother.

He applied salve on my wound, a slash at my right side just under the ribcage. It wasn't as bad as I had originally thought.

If it had been fatal, this would all be over. I could see brother again.

"*Ai-oh!*"

The heat from the soot he set aflame closed the wound.

Next thing I know, Eoha has me hoisted over his shoulder. He carried me all the way back to the cave, changing directions each time there was rustling in the bushes.

"I'm sorry." He used his *amip* to wipe away my tears. "We'll stay here for the night. I'll keep watch."

My hand gripped his wrist on instinct. "Stay."

He sat down next to me. "Okay."

"How many?" I asked, after sitting in silence till it hurt.

"Possibly three groups, maybe six men each. I can't be sure. I heard them, but I didn't see them."

I shook my head. "How many did you kill?"

Eoha looked down. "I'm…not sure."

"They are dead, right? You didn't just wound them? You made sure they were dead, right?"

Brother wanted them all dead. I do too.

"Ebui." He held me tightly.

"Horekeu. Isepo. What's the difference?"

His grip tightened.

"They killed him. They killed my…."

Eoha pressed his forehead against mine. "*Chishirikirap.*"

We sobbed in each other's arms.

As long as he's here, I can bear it. But how long before he is taken by fate?

"My…." My lips froze.

I can't say it. Why can't I say it?

I cleared my throat. "He left me with a mission."

"It isn't safe to go out right now. The Isepo chief is dead."

"Good."

That's all I could think to say about it. I once looked up to the man. There was even a time when I hoped the Shitumbe would follow his example of peace. I was so wrong.

"You shouldn't be moving around with that wound," he said, breaking apart from me to make some soup.

"Aren't the Isepo your friends?"

"Some of them are," he said before wiping his eyes.

That's right. That one Isepo warrior said he knew Eoha. He was banished...why was that again?

"This isn't the first time I've killed a friend." Eoha stirred the soup.

"I'm sorry. I...."

Why did I even ask? It was so cruel of me.

"I have no allegiance to the Isepo, you know that. Still, I need to know the mission you were left with."

"It's something I need to tell the chief."

Eoha sat next to me and held the soup bowl to my mouth. "Just take it slow, okay? What do you need to tell him? Can it wait till morning?"

I pulled away. "It was my brother's dying wish!"

The soup spilled on Eoha. I didn't even realize I knocked it out from his hands.

Eoha pressed his forehead to mine. He held me till I stopped shaking, and then got up to make more soup.

Was he really dead? Was my brother not coming back?

It felt like him and father had just gone away on a trip. Any moment they could arrive.

But they don't know where this cave is! I have to get home so they can find me!

"Ebui!"

I came back to my senses. I was standing at the cave exit. If there were Isepo or Horekeu nearby, they would no doubt have spotted me.

Eoha grabbed my hand. "You should get some rest."

"My mother. She doesn't know. She's waiting there all alone, not knowing where I am, where he is…when we'll come back…."

Eoha put his fingers over my lips. He seized my head and caressed my hair.

Each stroke took away a layer of worry. He tried to get me to sit down, but I didn't budge. "What if it's infected and I die before I can give the message?"

"Our best chance of survival is here. The wound is not infected. I made sure of it. Will you tell me what the message is?"

I looked into his amber eyes, so pure and well-intentioned.

So alive.

"The *tusu-guru* before me was poisoned by the Horokeu. It was at the bear ceremony of the Isepo clan. They sought to cripple my people by leaving them without a shaman. I'm their next target."

"The Horokeu didn't kill you so that they could use you as a bargaining chip to get the Isepo chief back, right? That means that the Isepo and the Horokeu have a strong alliance."

He figured all that out. Now for sure he won't let me leave.

"Ebui, this information will be just as useful tomorrow morning as it would be tonight. They are after you, you said so yourself. We should stay here."

"We need to prepare for war."

And kill every last one of them.

Eoha grabbed my hand. "Pan'ambe and Pen'ambe, the two foxes. One became rich. The other was impatient and is now poor."

Those are just stories. This is different.

"They want war. And we have no idea when they will attack," I said, my hand tightening into a fist and escaping his hold.

"The information is yours to pass on, and you will choose when to speak it. This is my advice; do with it what you will. There is distrust and panic in the air already. Telling the chief tonight or even tomorrow will only create more panic. Let us send off the dead. Once the village has calmed down, then I think you should tell the chief your message."

"You lied to me."

Eoha turned to me, his expression like a wounded dog.

"You said you have no allegiance to the Isepo. You don't want them to die, do you? You don't want my brother to rest in peace!"

"If the Shitumbe wage war against the Horokeu and the Isepo together, they will surely lose! I won't lose you," he said as firm as a mountain.

"You don't get it, do you?" I pushed him away. "My village will burn no matter what I do! I saw the broom star and then the vision came. All my visions have come true! Every, single, one!" I screamed out, not caring who heard me.

"What if...what if you only had that vision after seeing the *rikop* because you were scared? We don't know the future, Ebui. Every decision we make can change it."

"I hear teacher die and she died. I saw my brother die and he died! I thought becoming a *tusu-guru* would make sense of it all. I thought it would give me some control. But it hasn't! It's just made me realize how powerless I am!" I sobbed.

Eoha pushed me to the ground. He grabbed a spear by the side of the cave and ran off.

This was my chance.

I left, even though I knew it was wrong, and I knew he was in danger and that I was putting myself in harm's way. I don't know if it's because I was upset with him or scared he might convince me otherwise. Whether or not it had to do with the mission brother left me or my loyalty to my people– something I thought I had let go of.

Maybe brother's loyalty was passed down to me. Maybe his spirit is with me right now.

All I knew was that I had to return. Any doubt I had was buried and burned once I pictured the worry on mother's face.

It's okay, Mom. I'm coming home.

I arrived at my *chisei* without being spotted by anyone. Once I made it to the door I froze up.

How am I going to tell her?

I wasn't prepared. I hadn't rehearsed what to say. I hadn't figured out how to break the news. I was drawn there as a little girl seeking her mother's warmth. It was too soon after father's death. News of brother's death could make her ill.

I have a mission.

I turned away from the door.

Facing the chief and telling him the news didn't seem all that daunting in comparison. I had to fulfill my brother's wishes. This was more important than seeing my mother. I was the only *tusu-guru* my people had. I needed to take up teacher's mantle with pride.

Not sure whether I was really feeling that strong of a determination or if I was just too afraid to see Mom, I made my way to the chief's *chisei*.

I didn't even realize I was running.

If I get chastised for this, I'll end up crying again.

The noise woke up the chief. He sat up from his mat. "You've returned." He smiled.

"The bamboo-tipped arrows in my vision. It's true."

The chief's face went pale. "You're sure?" he asked, holding onto just a sliver of hope that maybe I had overlooked something.

"There were Isepo warriors working alongside the Horokeu. My brother uncovered their alliance after he captured a Horokeu spy in our village. Eikashu's death was not from the plague. He was poisoned at the Isepo bear ceremony."

The chief looked at me intensely and stood up. "Thank you for this information, Ebuike."

"That isn't all. My brother…."

"I shall inform the others in the morning. You are dismissed," said the chief.

"The morning? Look, the Isepo still have two sub-chiefs. If we form a night attack squad, we can find and kill the other chiefs. That will put their clan in disarray. Then when the Horokeu come to assist—"

The chief raised his hand. "I need my rest. You are dismissed."

Why isn't he more serious about this!?

I bowed and left walking backward, careful not to show any more offense than I already had.

I wiped my eyes.

Tears. He must have noticed. That's why he silenced me. Despite all I've done, he still treats me like a kid.

For some reason, I found myself smiling.

There was only one place left to go: home.

Once I arrived, I opened the door. She was standing just beyond the door. Before I knew it, her arms were holding me in a tight embrace.

"You shouldn't have run off without telling me. You worried me," she said, fixing my hair and dusting my *amip*. She noticed the cut. "What happened?"

I sat down on my mat. "I was attacked. Brother rescued me. Mom…." I wiped my tears. "He won't be coming home."

Her face contorted as she did her best not to cry. When she finally broke down, it came out as gurgled sobs.

It was my turn to comfort her.

I held her tightly and caressed her hair. I couldn't hold back my tears, but I stifled any sound that came out.

She was the babe now.

I found myself thinking back to my little bear cub, Noyuk.

Is that when it all went wrong?

I can't remember when I passed out, but I hope it was before mother did. I awoke the next morning.

I looked outside the window and saw some men gathered together.

They were the ones who were with brother!

With a sudden burst of energy I left my *chisei* and approached them. They were all alive, hardly wounded.

Why did they get to live and not him?

One of the men noticed me and signaled the others.

"What are you talking about, Isonash?" I asked, squeezing my way into their circle.

One of the men turned away. "We were so full of fury. We forgot our obligations to you. All of us ran off to kill the Isepo chief. At least two of us should have stayed behind. You were wounded and we left you."

"I needed to be alone. You did what had to be done," I said with newfound strength.

"It will not happen again. Two men at each side of your *chisei*, day and night. If you go out, we will escort you. And if—"

"Have you seen Eoha?"

"I do not know who that is." Isonash turned to the other men. They were equally confused.

"Of course you don't. My apologies. He is an outcast from the Isepo tribe. We met at Moyuk, the village of outcasts. He was the one who bandaged me up," I said, pointing to my wound.

"Ebuike, we have not seen him."

I froze up.

He couldn't be dead, could he?

"We have not informed the chief of the enemy alliance yet, but we will do so once he awakens. I recommend your friend stays away from this village. There is already suspicion toward the Isepo, and that will soon explode into hate once news of the alliance reaches our people. Right now we should all be care...." Isonash stopped mid-sentence.

Some men were rushing to the outskirts of the village. They were carrying spears.

The group of men I was talking to rushed ahead and I followed along.

At the foot of the hill we came to the source of the disturbance.

Eoha!

He was alive and well! He was also carrying something in an Isepo garment.

"Everyone, I am an outcast from the Isepo clan. I wish to join your tribe. May I speak with your chief?" asked Eoha, taking a step back once the spearmen approached.

"I am here," said the chief, coming up from behind me.

Eoha bowed. "Great *paunguru*. My name is Eoha. I offer up my allegiance to your tribe."

"Is he crazy?" "I don't trust him." "Could be a spy." Voices of ignorant men whispered gossip of suspicion.

The spearmen took another step toward Eoha.

I rushed in front of them, willing to get stabbed to keep him safe. "He is my friend. He saved my *ishu*."

The spearmen did not lower their weapons.

"What proof do you have that you are no longer a part of the Isepo?" asked the chief, having the spearmen step back once he approached.

Eoha opened up the garment and showed what was inside to the chief.

The chief's eyes widened.

I peeked over, getting an uncomfortably close look at the head of the youngest Isepo warrior.

The chief told Eoha to cover it up. He nodded to the spearmen. "We will welcome you into our tribe once the funeral ceremony is over. Come back tonight."

"My parents are still at the village. May they come too?"

"I will consider it," said the chief.

Eoha bowed, smiled at me, and then went into the forest.

"So you realize your people are the enemy now?" I asked.

"This head belonged to my friend. I found him fiercely wounded, but still alive. It was a mercy kill. Even in death he has helped me out. I thank him for helping me become welcomed into your village."

"He died attacking my brother. For all I know it was his spear that...."

My tears silenced me.

"Ebuike. You must lead the ceremony. Get some rest. We will start at sunset," said the chief before walking off.

Sunset came sooner than expected. I had gathered all of brother's *korobe* and placed them in a large box. I made sure everything, from the food to the placement of the hearth, was properly prepared for him.

I hope you're watching, brother.

As the people gathered, I placed some convolvulus roots near the fire to increase the heat.

Warmth is supposed to keep us from the coldness of death. But it couldn't do anything for him now. Nothing could.

The men came and brought his body—all dressed up in white—and placed it on the right side of the hearth.

Brother's flint, hunting knife, utensils, and cherished bow and arrow were placed at his side. A cup of boiled rice and some sake were placed near him so that he could take in their essence.

Brother was never much of a drinker.

I placed the *inao* around my brother's lifeless body. Even though it was time for me to speak, I froze up.

The chief noticed my hesitancy and spoke in my stead. "Atnep has left us. We gather here now to honor him and to bring his soul to the next world."

"We must burn away all his possessions so that he can move on, unattached," I said, unfolding his mat before tossing it in the fire.

After this is over, I won't be allowed to mention him. This is my last chance to share his story.

"Atnep was a rather difficult brother. He used to resent me because I was more attached to our second mom than our first. It's more than that…he blamed me for mother's death. I still loved him and I always admired his strength. But I thought he didn't love me. After I was banished, I think he realized how much he missed me. He had faith in me when I didn't, and he realized that I had nothing to do with mother's death. He came to bring me back home from banishment and on the way we finally connected. We were catching up on so many missed opportunities. He fought bravely till the very end. Atnep was one of the greatest warriors the Shitumbe have ever had. He was a great friend to so many. And even though I didn't realize it for many years, he was always a loving brother to me."

I kept my composure despite all the emotions swirling around inside me. "I beseech the goddess of fire to guide this spirit to the *kotan kara kamui*." I then began chanting.

Each trinket I tossed into the fire made me feel like I was losing another piece of him. I never thought his dirty bowl, his cup, and his other utensils would be so important to me. My hand shook as I tossed them in.

Brother's lifeless face was looking less familiar and more foreign by the second.

As I chanted, the ceremonial wine cup was passed around. Each person took a sip before offering three drops to my brother. Once the cup reached my lips, I could hardly see through my tears.

I closed my eyes, took a sip, gave him three drops, and offered the remainder of the wine to the *Abe Kamui*.

When the prayer and offerings were complete, two men wrapped my brother in a *toma* and attached his body to a pole. The men hoisted him up and began their journey to the spot where he was found.

The mourners, all women, followed in a single-file line, each bearing a small trinket to be buried along with him. The men, with spears raised, chanted *wool, wool, wool* all the way to the place he was killed.

When we arrived, the men smacked the surrounding area with their spears, chanting *wool, wool,* to scare off ill-intentioned spirits.

Brother was placed in the hole, still wrapped in the mat. The women broke the trinkets they brought with them and set them in the hole. The men then covered the hole with a slab of wood.

I turned away as my brother was buried under the dirt.

Despite all that happened, a part of me expected him to push off the mat and emerge from the pit.

Once the spear-like post was placed at the grave, with his headdress at the top, I had to accept it.

He was gone.

Not only was he gone, but I wouldn't even be permitted to visit this spot. Everyone would avoid it, avoid him. After all he's done for them, this tribe, and all he's done for me.

It isn't fair!

We returned to the village for *wen iku, wen ube.* After a funeral, the men would drink away their sorrows while the women wailed. Some of the mourners were faking, but some were genuinely shaken up by his loss. A few of brother's close friends gathered around to share tales of his bravery and of his *ishu* in general. Apparently he talked about me all the time and he looked up to me.

If I only I knew sooner. I can never gain back the lost time between us.

When the scent of sake became too strong for me, I prepared to leave.

Also, I didn't want to hear about brother killing a mother bear.

Noticing I was sneaking away, the chief called everyone to attention. "I have important news to share." After he made sure everyone's eyes were fixed on him, he cleared his throat. "The Isepo have allied with the Horokeu, and the Isepo chief was killed by one of our own. We must stay vigilant at all times."

"Great chief, what is our plan of action?" I asked.

"We must be wary of our actions. The Horokeu are strong on their own, and the Isepo are clever. We cannot win a fight against both of them."

"Then I will lead a party to kill the Isepo's sub-chiefs. That will throw them in disarray."

"We cannot solve this problem with violence. If we fight, we will lose. We must try to negotiate with the Horokeu."

"They killed my brother!" I yelled. Noticing my outburst, I took a step back and lowered my head. "They poisoned our shaman."

Gasps and exclamations of horror erupted from the crowd.

"Ebuike, I have a responsibility to our people. I'd rather bow to the enemy than be annihilated by them."

"Please, chief, allow me and a small group to attack," said brother's closest friend.

"Absolutely not. We will not engage in combat unless we are attacked. The sub-chiefs and I have decided upon the proper course of action to take. I will leave in the morning to negotiate a treaty between us."

I couldn't listen anymore. I ran off, else I would have surely lost my composure.

The chief wants to befriend our enemies. Brother wanted every Isepo dead. I won't give up on his wish.

The next morning, Eoha was welcomed to our village—though not without some difficulty. Many of the men and women didn't trust him because he was once Isepo, but after showing them the head of an Isepo warrior, both him and his parents were welcomed in. The chief made sure each of them had a place before he left with a small group for negotiations. After wishing him a safe journey and making several offerings for his sake, I waved farewell to the chief and rushed to Eoha.

I was rather nervous when Eoha introduced me to his parents. They were very kind and rather fond of me. There were no doubts that Eoha already spoke with them about his plans to marry. At dinner the mother mentioned that my cooking skills would make me a great wife someday, and the father said he hopes his son will find a girl so beautiful.

After dinner, Eoha and I led them to their *chisei*—an elderly couple said that they were welcome to stay with them. Eoha and I went back to my home.

Finally, I had a chance to speak with him one-on-one.

I found myself in his arms before I realized it. "I missed you," I said, clenching him tightly.

"I am here now." He kissed my forehead.

"That Isepo warrior, did you kill him? What I mean is…were you possessed?"

"He had located us. I didn't have a choice. I don't regret it. Came out rather handy in the end."

"Did you know him?"

I immediately regretted asking the question once it left my lips.

Eoha broke the embrace and placed his hands on my shoulders. "I will do whatever I need to do in order to be with you."

I leaned in and kissed his lips.

"Have you thought about my proposal?" he asked, kissing my neck.

"Yes," I said, pulling back a bit while caressing his sides.

"And?" His warm hands touched my cheek.

"I need more time to think."

"Of course. You've been through so much," he said, holding me in his arms.

"Eoha, if there is a war, I want to fight. Will you fight with me?"

"The chief will do all he can to prevent a war."

"But there's no point! It's going to happen and likely in just a few years."

"Then we must prepare. I'll ask one of the men to train us."

"Good."

"Ebui, can I sleep with you tonight?"

"Please do," I said, grasping his hand.

How long before I lose him too?

Chapter 6: Union & Separation

The chief never came back. To make recompense for the killing of the Isepo chief, he gave up his life. The peace between our tribes was further maintained by giving up a portion of our harvest—fifteen percent to the Isepo and twenty-five percent to the Horokeu. We were no longer proud foxes. We had been reduced to beggars. My brother sought the Isepo's annihilation, and I wouldn't let anything get in the way of his wishes. Eoha and I trained to be great warriors. The peace treaty between the tribes went on for two long years, but the trees were growing. My prophecy was looming closer each day.

"Nice catch," said one of the men, referring to the way I had thrust my spear through a particularly large trout.

My mind flashed to the time I shot the squirrel with my brother, like it often did.

The old me was afraid of killing. That child didn't have the fortitude to do what had to be done for my people. With nearly half our harvest handed over as a peace offering, we did more gathering and, of course, more hunting as well. I was a woman now and a blooming warrior. I wasn't the only woman learning to hunt either. More and more were realizing that the treaty would not last.

I had become skilled at killing in such a short time. Each time I released an arrow or thrust my spear, I pictured the face of one of the men who killed my brother. It was a surefire way to remove any hesitation.

I looked into the pain in the fish's eyes. He flapped around, hoping by a miracle to escape the spear. But even if he did somehow escape the iron tip, he would surely die from blood loss.

I never did grow out of my paranoia. After any kill I would always remove the eyes of the victim, that way their spirit wouldn't recognize me.

"Are you sure you don't want any?" asked one of the men, scaling his most recent catch.

"The *moshiri ikkew kepp* is a trout on which every island resides. I don't want to anger him by eating his offspring," I said.

"If you don't want to kill them, you don't have to. We can reach our quota on our own," said one of the men.

"I must prepare each and every day for what is to come," I said, removing my catch's eyes before tossing him to one of the men.

"A storm will be coming soon. We should dock and wait it out," said Eoha, standing at the bow of our boat.

"A storm, after all the offerings you gave them?" asked one of the men.

"Perhaps I should offer more," said Eoha, starting to carve more *inao*.

"Why not? Though it seems *Shi-Acha* has been overtaking *Mo-Acha* this season," said one of the men.

"I don't think that's it. They're playing with us, the both of them. One wants to be revered and the other feared. The eldest *kamui* is no more evil than his younger brother," I said, glaring at the sky.

"*Mo-Acha* stops storms and makes sure we arrive safely. How is he as bad as the storm bringer? You should be careful what you say," said the man.

"I think *Mo-Acha* is the crueler of the two brothers. He gives us hope and then has his elder brother dash it to pieces. Besides, who's to say *Shi-Acha* isn't just trying to protect the *chep* from us?" I asked before obtaining another kill.

"That's right. To the Ainu, *Mo-Acha* is a guardian, but to the trout, *Shi-Acha* is a guardian. This world is a series of islands surrounded by one interconnected body of *aka*. Each island holds its own viewpoint. As do the fish, the bears, the Shitumbe, and the other tribes. Good and evil is just a matter of perspective," said Eoha, putting his arm around me.

He's wrong. The Isepo and the Horokeu are both evil. And they will both be dealt with.

We docked at the beach, near the forest surrounding our village.

"We're going to collect some berries. Carry on without us once the storm is done," said Eoha, grabbing my hand.

"Be careful and don't get near the border. We've lost four women to the Horokeu this season," said the man.

"We will stay vigilant." Eoha turned to me. "There isn't a storm coming, is there?"

"Maybe not," I said, connecting my fingers behind my back.

"You miss him, don't you?"

"I nodded."

Hand in hand we made it to brother's burial spot.

It was *hatto-an* to visit a burial site, but I wasn't afraid. Not because I had thought brother's spirit had already moved on. On the contrary, I felt safe because I could always feel his presence there.

"Hello brother. Sorry I haven't visited in a while. It's been difficult to break apart from the group. But now that I am here, I have good news. The men are getting restless. I doubt the peace treaty will last the rest of the season."

"Is that really what you want?" asked Eoha, looking at me with worry.

"It's what you want, isn't that right, brother? As you know, Eoha and I have been training a lot. I've heard killing a man is different than killing an animal, but in the end it's all about tearing through flesh and bone. And most *chikoikip* are cleverer than the Horokeu, so I'm not too worried. Of course, I'll be careful. But I'm getting a bit restless myself. Hopefully the chief will end the treaty soon. I promise, when the time comes, their blood will be spilt. The forest will be washed in it, and then the Shitumbe can be free. Sorry I can't stay for long, but the others are already a bit suspicious. I know it's been so long, but soon you'll be able to rest."

"I will keep your sister safe. I will fulfill my promise to you," said Eoha with a bow.

"Farewell for now, brother." I grabbed Eoha's hand and rushed down to the lake.

He was so handsome.

Eoha had grown in the last two years but still had a rounded childish face. His arms were muscular, though not like brother's were. Black hair went over the left side of his face like a quarter moon, giving him a mysterious charm. Most importantly, his amber eyes gazed at me with love and respect. They didn't mirror his carefree spirit like they used to.

We stripped down and washed each other in the cool water. "You don't really think we're contaminated by his spirit, do you?"

Eoha smiled. "I don't, but it's always good to be careful. Spirits have powerful energy."

I turned around and kissed him. "Is that the only reason?"

"I'd be a fool to miss an opportunity to wash you," said Eoha.

117

We got out of the bath, and he beat my back with *inao* to dispel any negative energy still clinging to me. Once finished, he handed me the *inao* and turned around.

He has such a cute butt.

Once we were sure the other was clean, we dressed each other.

"As beautiful as ever, *chiri-po*," he said, his arm over my shoulder.

I looked into the lake and gazed at my reflection.

I was still shorter than him, though the difference was almost negligible now. I proudly wore the dress my mother made, which displayed my devotion to my tribe with an embroidered Shitumbe pattern. My long brown *attush*, made from the inner bark of elm trees, was held together with shells– one of which was given to me by my beloved. My hair came out from beneath my headdress. It was long and flowing, defiantly branching out in multiple directions. The sooty, dark blue tattoo mark around my lips was accentuated by my rosy cheeks. My blue eyes sparkled like the stars in the night sky. The beaded necklace my mother made me kept me from ever feeling lonely. The special charm, attached to a second necklace, was given to me by Eoha for my protection and as part of a promise two years ago.

"Only a few more cycles now," he said, jiggling my charm and caressing my hair.

"Yeah, it's getting hard to hold back," I said, leaning into him.

Eoha blushed and nodded.

So cute.

"You sure made it difficult," he said with a smirk.

He was right. I did.

About half a year after the chief left to negotiate, Eoha finally got me to accept. It was on the day of the bear sacrifice, no less. He proposed to me once the bear cub had been taken out to be killed. I was shocked at the time, but with such a large crowd I couldn't say no. I don't even know why it took me so long to agree. Anyways, after proposing, he told Noyuk's story. After hearing about my love for the little bear and to celebrate our future union, the bear cub was set free. Many of the girls and some of the women even protested against the cruelty of such a ceremony, though the men weren't as understanding. I had never been so moved by Eoha before. Sometimes I wonder if he's too good for me.

We returned to the village.

A man came up to us. He informed us of the situation and led us to the *chisei*.

Eoha's father was pale in the face.

"Father, when did you start feeling ill?" asked Eoha.

"A few days ago. I didn't think anything of it at the time," said the patient, his face a bit pale.

"He has been cursed," I said softly.

A few months ago, Eoha's father was cursed. We couldn't locate the culprit, but it was likely one of the men who still refuses to accept him. What's strange is there were quite a few cases of others trying to curse me, yet I haven't been plagued by illness since I returned from the village of outcasts. The *kamui* have other plans for me, it seems.

Eoha and I worked together to drive away the curse and within only a few days the father had recovered. Working along with our close friends, we tracked down the perpetrator.

119

We placed some wine at the East end of the *chisei* for our ancestors and headed out.

Four men were each holding a string attached to a fox skull. When there are multiple culprits, the *shitumbe marapto* or ceremony of the fox, is the preferred way of determining the perpetrator. Each man pulled a string. The one responsible, made apparent by the skull's jaw falling facedown, was promptly tied up.

I was surprised it was Isonash. I thought when he warned me not to bring Eoha here, he was concerned for his safety. Then again, he was even more open about killing the Isepo than I was. He was a close friend to my brother and blames the Isepo for his death. After his wife vanished near the border, he has been doing all he could to rally the others to break the treaty. He had already been beaten with a club for his first offense: being caught near Eoha's parents' home after dark.

Such a shame. He could have been useful.

His arm was placed in boiling water. I never heard a man scream so loud.

"Let's go," said Eoha, grabbing my arm.

"He caused harm to your father. Don't you want to watch him receive judgment?"

"I do not. Why do you, Ebui? Us watching won't change his sentence. Father is safe," said Eoha.

"He'll curse your father again unless he learns his lesson. I want to make sure he has a change of heart."

The man screamed as the heated stone was placed in his hands. If his hands were burnt, that would prove his guilt. Then he would have to confess. If he is lucky he won't get banished, but considering this is his second offense, I'm pretty sure we won't be seeing him again.

"I'm going to see how the harvest is doing," said Eoha, walking away.

I chased after him. "Did I upset you?"

Eoha cleared his throat. "That man is a Shitumbe; he isn't our enemy."

"Anyone who threatens my family is my enemy. How can you be so forgiving?"

Eoha's father and I had gotten rather close. He was like a second father to me. Our mothers got along too.

"You've changed so much. I don't think your brother would want to see how vengeful you've become."

"He is still here because I haven't fulfilled my promise to him. My brother won't move on until all of them are dead."

"He's watching over you. That's why he is staying."

"You don't know him like I do."

"The Isepo will be coming in a few weeks. If you wear your hatred of them on you, they will notice. Our marriage can mend the tension between the two clans. We must be careful of our thoughts just as much as our actions," said Eoha, placing his arm around me.

"I don't want peace."

"I know. But let's make it last as long as it can," he said, kissing my forehead.

I turned away from him, unable to agree.

Two weeks came and went. After much preparation and anticipation, the day of our wedding had arrived. It was three days after I turned sixteen. I already felt like a woman, but the marriage added a new layer of purpose to my growth. My mother prepared me a special soup in the morning. After breakfast, Eoha's mom and my mother dressed me up.

On the way to the ceremony, I saw a young boy scaring away a crow. "Go away, it's my bread," he said with a grimace.

I bent down to the child. "You should not complain about any living being. They all have a purpose."

"What purpose? All they do is steal from us."

"The crows take what they have earned. It was a crow that flew into the Nitne Kamui's mouth to save the sun."

"Yeah, yeah, but what about mosquitoes? They're a total nuisance," said the boy.

"Be wary of what you say. Mosquitoes only take a little bit of blood. Hobgoblins take blood, flesh, and bone. You should not complain about such small problems."

The boy crossed his arms. "Okay."

"The evil one spoke of the bramble bush being superfluous, and then his tongue was eaten by a rat. We must be respectful."

The boy nodded with some hesitancy. "You're right."

"I'm sure you'll make a great mother," said the boy's mom.

"Thank you," I said, with a blush.

I love children, but I could never be a mother. What if my child was taken from me? Or what if they were born with the same burden of dark premonitions?

"You look *shiretok*." I turned around to see Eoha all dressed up for the ceremony. Just like me, he had a new garment specifically embroidered for this occasion.

Mother joined me and together we distributed the millet and rice cakes we had made the other day. Eoha and his father gave out the rice wine. We then joined in the center and held hands.

"My son has found his other half. His bride is so beautiful and intelligent. As his father, I couldn't be happier. The two of them will surely bring about great change." Eoha's father stepped up to his son. "I present the groom with the family *aumshup*, passed down for eight generations." He handed him an antique bow, complete with a quiver full of bamboo-tipped arrows.

Eoha bowed to his father.

Shitumbe and Isepo both cheered.

The Isepo men seemed so calm and good natured. No. I know what they have done and what they will do to my people.

I noticed a small Isepo girl hoisted on her mother's shoulder.

They have a family. Should I really wipe them out?

My mother touched my shoulder, bringing me back to my senses. She placed grandmother's earrings in my hands.

Orange and shaped like a curled up fox. They were so cute.

It was usually the shaman's job to make the *inao*, but since we were the ones being married, the men of the Shitumbe and Isepo prepared them beforehand.

Eoha and I offered the *inao* to many deities, asking for their permission.

Would the gods allow for the ceremony to complete? Would they really let me find happiness? If so, how long before it would be taken from me?

Once the offerings were completed, we came back to the center.

"Ebui, I first noticed you when I saw your face. But I fell in love when I saw how much you cared for that little bear. You're the light of my *ishu*. You saved me when I was banished, you gave me a home, and most importantly, you returned my love. This is the most memorable moment of my life. You are my bride forevermore."

"Eoha, you fought to save Noyuk, my little boy. I may have nursed you back to health, but you've freed me from my curse. This is a prophecy we made together, and I hope that it is only the start of many more miracles. You are now my husband. I'll never leave your side."

I placed my head against his chest and he held me dearly.

Songs, dancing, wine, and revelry filled the rest of the night. After finishing my meal with my new family, I grabbed my husband's hand. The main ceremony was completed, so Eoha and I got up, bowed to the chiefs and left.

Once inside the cabin we became locked in a passionate kiss. I stripped him down as he stripped me, rejoining to kiss the moment our garments were removed.

My hands moved up his sides.

He grabbed me and laid me on the mat. His kisses traveled up my thighs all the way to my neck.

The gentle kisses sent surges of passion through my body.

He rubbed my thighs as our noses pressed together. "We did it, *chiri-po*. We created our own future." A loving *chopchose* was placed on my forehead.

"I've figured it out." My hands went up his sides and caressed his chest. "This is the promise you made him. If he was going to entrust me to you, he needed you to marry me. Brother wanted to make sure you were serious about your feelings for me. That's why you were so pushy, wasn't it?" I asked, fiddling around with his ear.

Eoha smiled and lowered himself so he was lying at my side. "That isn't it, Ebui. I promised that I would convince you to bear a child." His placed his hand just below my belly.

Of course! I should have figured it out sooner!

"It would be irresponsible of me to have a child," I said, turning away.

"I would never force you to do something you were uncomfortable with. Your brother knew how much you love children, and he wanted to prove you aren't cursed. I didn't even bother to bring it up because we hadn't married yet. This marriage was a prophecy we created. Now that it has come to fruition, we can start a new prophecy," he said, caressing my hair.

I do want a child. I've looked forward to being a mother for so long.

"What if something bad happens?" I asked softly.

"You don't have to be afraid. If you want a child, then you should have one. You deserve it, Ebui. The *kamui* won't deny you lasting happiness. Our marriage proves this, does it not?"

I turned to him, tears welling up in my eyes. "Don't you see? They want to give me hope before taking it all away. They only permitted our union

125

so they could break us apart. If by some miracle I become pregnant, then it will bring about either my own end or the demise of our child."

Eoha held me tightly. "There's always a chance of that happening, but wouldn't you rather take the chance than regret not doing so your whole life? I want to raise a family with you. I want to prove that we can both be happy."

"It will end as a tragedy. I just know it."

"When was the last time you had a grim prophecy?"

"Two years ago," I said softly.

"Exactly. The stars have shifted. We are free to forge our own path."

"We are not. The village will soon burn. Nothing can stop it."

Eoha grabbed my hand. "We will deal with that if and when it comes up. When we dwell on negative things we give them power. Why not think positive thoughts instead."

"Whenever I hope for a future, that's when things fall apart."

"Our marriage was a success," he said, kissing my hand.

"Yeah."

"I've told you my feelings. But I can't change yours. This is something we must both agree on. Would you like to get some rest?"

He's so sweet.

"I want to be with you," I said with a smile.

He kissed me deeply.

I love him so much.

"We don't need children to be happy. Perhaps you should become a teacher. After all, you don't need to birth a child in order to be a mother. We can take in one of the orphans. Perhaps that is best," he said, rubbing his nose against my cheek.

"Yes, that sounds wonderful."

"You are so very beautiful."

I gripped his sides. "But I want two kids." I peeked up at him with a reluctant smile.

"We can adopt two."

I pressed up against him. "I want one child to come from our union."

Eoha blushed bright red. "Are you sure?"

Despite all my worries, I nodded.

Side by side we joined together. We moved as one.

"Wait. It hurts a bit," I said, slightly pulling out.

It didn't hurt at all. It felt amazing. I'm still a bit worried, that's all.

"Whenever you are ready," he said, combing a lock of hair away from my eyes.

I took a deep breath. "Okay. I'm ready."

Eoha gripped my sides and turned us so that I was on top of him. "Take it at your own pace."

I kissed his cheek.

Was it too late to quit? Maybe I should tell him to stop.

"Creation is an act that takes two. If only the woman or man made children, they would be no different than that parent. It is the melding of two bodies, two minds that becomes something wholly unique. Without uniqueness, it is not creation. If you are worried, then we can stop. If we do make a child, I want that moment to be full of love and passion, and free of doubt."

"I love you," I said softly, gazing into his eyes.

"I love you too," he said with a blissful smile.

I moved my body up and down. The two of us squirmed around until his hopes burst inside me. We lay in each other's arms, kissing until we fell asleep.

That night we made a new prophecy for a better future. I went to sleep hoping that the *kamui* wouldn't interfere with our happiness.

Chapter 7: Loss & Emptiness

We decided to wait on adopting until we had our first child. That way we could have both a boy and a girl. Four months passed and I fell ill, despite having a protective *chikappo*.

All the charms in the world couldn't keep me safe.

My husband found an effigy of me placed upside-down in a hole by the east end of the village. Someone wanted me gone. Even after the effigy was removed, I didn't recover.

There were quite a number of men who opposed Eoha's union with me, so it took some time before the suspect was found. It was four days into my illness, after my husband and I took a bath in the lake near my brother's grave post, when my *amip* were stolen. My husband tracked down the perpetrator, retrieved my clothes—which thankfully hadn't been cut—and brought him in for judgment and punishment.

My illness worsened despite the source of it being uprooted. Two weeks later, my water broke.

My husband rushed to my side. Considering how soon it was, we both knew the baby wouldn't make it. My husband held my hand and sang to me.

"The bunny was lost in the rain. Lost in the rain...."

After singing me the song I once sang to him, my husband informed me of the recent developments. The other tribes increased the amount they usually confiscated from our harvest. Eoha told me this with a concerned look. As for me, well, I couldn't hide my smile. This was what was necessary to push the Shitumbe to fight back. My only hope was that I would be in good health before war was declared. I looked forward to the day I would be back on my feet and cutting down Horokeu and Isepo alike.

Four days later, the illness had passed.

My husband sat by my side at dinner-time. "Ebui, I can't express my regret over what happened."

It was strange. I know he meant what he said, but he was so relieved I had recovered that he was smiling at the time.

I grabbed his hand. "It was our decision."

"Either way, our child is lost…and I almost lost you," he embraced me and cried against my shoulder.

"Just promise you'll trust me next time. If we try again, it will just end up the same."

"Miscarriages happen. This has nothing to do with a curse."

"You have no way of knowing that," I said with a firm tone.

"Did you have a vision?" he asked softly.

I turned away. "No. I didn't."

No doubt if I had tried to see the future, I would have known my child would die.

My eyes shrank.

Even without trying to see my future, prophesized events still occur. I cannot escape this curse.

"If you didn't, then they are unrelated," said Eoha.

"Are you certain?" I asked, my gaze intensifying.

"It matters not. Both of us agree that trying again would put you at risk. Take it easy, and perhaps in a few days we can pick out a child from the orphans."

"No. After what happened, I cannot. I will not tie anyone else to my fate."

"Bearing a child was supposed to break you free from paranoia," cried Eoha.

"Instead I hope it brings you to accept reality. There is no way for me to escape misfortune. I'm not allowed to be happy," I said.

"Get some rest, *chiri-po*. I must attend the meeting to discuss our village's next course of action."

That night I dreamt of a *kunne* cave, screams, and blood.

In three days I had fully recovered from my illness. Things between the Shitumbe and the two tribes had reached the tipping point. Young men were being trained for battle. In the dark of night, the men would gather. The chief seemed unaware, or perhaps he knew there was nothing he could do to stop it. One night I came into the room full of men.

The men stood at attention. "Great shaman. What are you doing here?" they asked, one of them casually putting away the war plans.

"I am here on behalf of the *paunguru*. Your actions could bring about a war," I said, walking to one of the men and seizing the plans.

"The elder does not know what is best for the village. His fixation with peace will bring about our destruction," said the shortest of the men.

"You best watch your tongue and show *uainu* to your elders. After all, they may be the great Okikurumi in disguise," I said, overlooking the plans.

None of it made sense to me. I wasn't sure what tribe was which symbol. I assumed the pointed shapes were archers, but even that was just a guess.

"Perhaps that's the problem. Okikurumi founded all the tribes, not just our own," said one of the men under his breath.

"He no longer sees things as we do. His ascension has left him blinded by our plight. Despite him having the best intentions, he has led us down a path of ruin," I said.

"We are in agreement. What is the problem then?" asked the leader.

"I want in on these meetings, and I want to be trained in the art of warfare."

"Absolutely not. You are our *tusu-guru*; you are far too important to be risked in battle."

"If we don't win, then we'll all be killed. War makes everyone into equals," I said, picking up a spear that was leaned against the wall.

"I know you've been hunting with us, but this is different," said the tall man.

"Let me prove myself," I said, gripping the spear with both hands.

"You are not your brother," said the leader.

"Three men. All I ask for is three men to accompany me to the caves. I will slay a bear. That will prove I am capable of fighting our enemies," I said.

"And if you fail, we will be left with only one shaman," said the leader.

"I've seen past that moment. In my vision, I stood alongside the men, cutting down a treacherous Isepo spearman."

I hadn't really had that vision, but they didn't need to know that.

"Even so—"

"If I die, then my premonition was incorrect and I would have been worthless to my people as a shaman. I will not fail," I said, staring into the leader's eyes with my brother's strength.

"I'll go. Who else will come along?" asked the leader.

My hunting captain stepped up, as did one of his subordinates.

"Tell the chief it is time to prepare for another bear ceremony," said the leader.

"How wonderful. All the tribes will come to attend." I handed the leader the plans. "It will certainly be an unforgettable day."

He smiled at me. "We leave first thing in the morning. Get some rest, men," said the leader.

I nodded and went back to my *chisei*, cuddled up to Eoha, and fell asleep.

When the sun rose I snuck out, careful not to wake my husband.

Even when sleeping he is so handsome. I hope he doesn't worry too much when he can't find me.

The men were just outside the western entrance to the village. They were playing *ukara*.

The leader's back was hit sixteen times with a club. He raised his hand, signaling the man to stop. Once he noticed me, I saw a slight smile form on his face. "Come, join us."

"Isn't that a game for men?" I asked.

"It's for warriors," he said, hitting his chest with a firm fist.

Most of the men snickered and whispered as I stepped up.

The leader raised his club to my back and struck it seven times. I knew he was holding back, and I was impressed at how he hit so softly while appearing to hit hard. Even so, it hurt a lot. As he pulled back for the eighth, I raised my hand.

"Seven hits. Not bad," he said, slugging my arm.

One of the men, likely with a lower score, stepped up. "You weren't hitting at full force."

"Is that so? Come up and see for yourself," he said, raising the club.

The man smiled awkwardly and stepped back.

I approached the leader. "Why are there six? I said I only needed three."

"As long as you're the one who makes the kill, you've proven yourself. The more men there are, the less likely any of us will die. Follow me."

With me staying behind, the hunters received the chief's *inunuke*. After they met up with me, we asked protection from the gods: for the mountains to lead us and for the river to carry us safely, as well as for the spring to nourish us, and the fire to keep us warm. We then ventured into the forest. The trek to the mountain took three days and another to scale it. At each rest spot we paid tribute to the local deities. When it was my shift for night watch, the leader would always join me. He was so fascinated by my stories. I had assumed men like him were only interested in bragging about their exploits. His calm but powerful demeanor kept me at ease. And hearing about the times he took down a bear helped prepare me for what was to come. Despite this, I froze up when we arrived at the bear's den.

"Stay focused," he said, bringing me back with a touch to my shoulder.

I pressed my feet deep into the snow, trying to find some firm footing.

The leader signaled two men to get on each side of the cave and prod it with their spears. Since the bear did not come out, the leader smoked it out with a torch.

Big bear.

It was even bigger when it stood up on its hind legs.

Here I am, doing something I know is wrong and dangerous. But I'll do what I have to.

One of the men jabbed his spear at the bear. With a single whack, the spear snapped. Another whack and the man was on the ground with blood spilling out from his garments.

I raised my bow and fired the poisoned-tipped arrow into the bear's neck.

I know it was typical for bear hunts, but, using poison made me feel awful. My father was poisoned by the Horokeu, and I always saw it as a tool for cowards.

One of the men rushed behind the bear, grabbed the spear he left on the ground and pierced the bear's back.

The spear bore fairly deep before the man holding it lost his grip and fell down.

The leader rushed at the bear with a small knife, howling at it to give it even the slightest intimidation.

I fired an arrow at its side before his dagger pierced its chest. He ripped the dagger out and leaped back, just barely dodging a swipe aimed at his head. One of the men who plunged his spear into its belly was not so lucky. A single strike to the head snapped the man's neck. His face contorted into a gruesome display of pain.

This was what war was like. Alive one moment, dead the next. Crucial decisions and moments of instinctual insight. It could end right here. Then I wouldn't have to see the village burn. But it would still burn, and my brother's spirit would linger.

I raised my bow and fired another shot, and another, and another. I had gotten the bear's attention.

The leader sliced the bear's side, causing blood to gush out.

I dropped my bow.

A swipe to the head, my neck twisted, and I fall dead.

I never expected to have a premonition like this, in a moment of life and death.

I ducked the inevitable swipe and plunged my dagger into the bear's throat.

The leader, along with the other men, pierced it from behind.

The bear wailed in pain, crying like a child before falling over dead.

There was no cheering. The men rushed to their fallen comrades. One was gravely injured and the other clearly dead. It took me a moment to recognize him. It was the one who taught Eoha and I how to *emoni*. Of course he would be the one to die.

Seems my curse is still alive.

It didn't bother me. I didn't feel much of anything. I wasn't sad or angry. It wasn't even that I expected him to die. I guess after losing so many, he had just become another. Besides he was a hunter, killing was his *ishu*. It seemed unfair to feel sorry for him.

The leader and the men turned the bear over, said their prayers, and began carving. Once the bear was skinned, I offered *inao* to the gods.

What gods were protecting the bear from us? Do bears give praise when they successfully defend their homes from invaders?

Many questions bounced in my head as I paid tribute.

"You've earned this," said the leader, handing me the bear's head.

"I don't want that. I want to be trained as a soldier, that's all."

"You've proven yourself worthy. The one who deals the final blow receives the head and—"

"We all made the kill. Are there cubs inside?" I asked, walking past the eating men.

Four small bears came out from the cave. They went to their downed mother and solemnly licked her wounds.

I wiped my tears and took a deep breath. "We should take the oldest one," I said, my voice cracking.

The leader and three men tied up the largest of the cubs, and we began our journey home.

That night, the leader and I kept watch. I was hoping for a confrontation. Poison arrows were best used against the Horokeu, anyway.

"I knew those men very well," he said in a gentle voice I wasn't aware he was capable of making.

"*Chishirikisap.*"

"You knew Raiochi as well."

"Yeah, I did," I said, trying to sound sad.

"Yet you are unfazed by his loss."

"I've grown accustomed to it."

He placed his hand on mine. "You are unlike any woman. You have power, skill, intelligence, and beauty."

I pulled my hand away. "And I have a loving husband."

Is this why he agreed to my terms? To swoon me?

"Haha. It is common for a man to have many wives. But it is unheard of for a shaman to be a woman. You broke a tradition. Perhaps we can break another." His hand climbed up my side.

I grabbed his arm and glared at him. "I'm not interested."

"A shame. The women in our village are too timid for me. Either too timid or too talkative. Are you sure?"

"Last night I had a vision of a man who was too pushy. He grabbed a woman in the dark and was poisoned by an arrow."

"Okay. I understand. Oh well, I suppose I'll have to keep searching."

That night I realized just how much I missed Eoha. There isn't a single man I'd rather be around.

But the more I love him, the more likely he is to die.

We made it back to the village and shared the meat in silence.

When one of our own dies, there is no retelling of the adventure, the feast is done in mourning. Supposedly the *ibehe* loses its flavor, but it tasted the same to me.

Eoha saw me and met me with a warm embrace.

"I missed you too," I said, kissing his cheek.

"What were you thinking?"

"I wanted to be a warrior."

"You could have been killed."

I lifted my shirt and turned around. "No injuries, see?"

"What are you planning to do at the bear ceremony?"

How did he figure me out?

"I'm not sure I follow."

"The Horokeu and the Isepo will be there. What are you planning to do?"

"Nothing," I said with a shrug.

It was true. I didn't quite have a plan of action yet. I wanted to discuss things with the other men. Judging by the size of the cub, the ceremony would take place in a month. It was more than enough time to figure out how to deal with my enemies.

My village will burn and many will die. I'll just have to make sure more of them die than us.

Chapter 8: Fire & War

I went through intensive training for several months. I became a full-fledged warrior, though still a fresh one. Before I knew it, the day of the bear ceremony had arrived. I had discussed my plans with my allies in advance. I also made sure to mix the poisons properly. Getting the balance right so it would kill, but not immediately, was very tricky.

The ceremony started out as usual. It pained me to watch it. But I would only have a chance to deliver the poisoned drinks after the bear cub was killed. Even more than the abuse of the bear cub, it was the anticipation of seeing the enemy chiefs dying that made me restless.

The little bear cried out for its mother as it died.

>*Shut up! Just go away already!*

I hated the wretched sounds it made.

I passed out the wine and watched, though not in a suspicious manner, as the chiefs of both the Horokeu and the Isepo emptied the cups.

After the food was finished, one of the chiefs stood up. He said he was tired and wanted to rest here for the night. Our chief gladly agreed.

As the Horokeu chief walked to his temporary abode, he collapsed.

>*It wasn't supposed to happen this soon.*

A Horokeu shaman went to his fallen chief's side. The color in his face died out.

Before he could say 'poison' we attacked.

Grabbing our hidden spears we rushed at the enemy.

I rammed my spear into a Horokeu and kept pushing till it pierced through an Isepo.

This is for my brother!

Twelve men and I took out thirty-three enemies in a rush of adrenaline.

"Ebui, stop!" yelled Eoha.

The tip of my spear was resting in the chest of an Isepo woman.

I saw the fear in my victim's eye and froze up. She was indeed Horokeu, but all I saw was a terrified woman.

One of the men finished what I had started. "We cannot let them flee!" After finishing off one of the women, he rushed into a group of four that were sprinting to the trees for safety.

They were all killed in a matter of seconds.

I turned and wretched.

Every one of them must die. Why am I feeling this way?

"Tie up the shaman. We can use him to bargain back our freedom," said the leader.

Eoha picked me up and took me back to our cabin. "Why did you do this?"

"The fire will happen. Our people will be killed and our village will burn. I can't stop my premonitions from happening, but I can make sure they happen on my terms."

"They will retaliate and soon. Pack up tonight. I won't lose you to this war. We leave in the morning."

141

"You want me to abandon my people?"

"By inciting war, you've already abandoned your people! The Shitumbe will be wiped out. We must go to Moyuk. We'll be safe there."

"I'm not afraid of death."

"How would your brother feel if you died?"

"How would he feel if I fled? I will stay and fight."

"You will be killed."

"Then I die a warrior."

Eoha embraced me. "Please, Ebui…."

"You should go. This was my premonition and my plan. I'll handle the consequences."

"I'm staying." Eoha kissed my cheek.

"Okay."

With our chief having fled, the new chief decided everyone must be trained to fight. Every able-bodied man, woman, and child found a weapon they could handle and learned to wield it. When they attacked, we would be ready.

One, then two, then four weeks passed, and no word from our enemy. We stayed focused.

The day they would come to collect our harvest was in three days. That night, I heard a horrible noise.

"Wool! Wool!" chanted a man.

The smell of smoke filled the air.

I looked outside my window.

I saw Eoha fighting an Isepo spearman before the battle went beyond my field of vision.

I rushed out of my *chisei*, not even thinking of grabbing a weapon. As I came to help, I caught a glimpse of Eoha's eyes. They were cold and vacant. He sliced through three enemies and sped into another group.

I was caught up in a night raid. Fire, bodies pierced with bamboo-tipped arrows—the prophesized catastrophe had arrived. Bows, sticks, stones, clubs, men fighting men, women fighting women, even children picking up what they could find to attack other children—it was all-out war.

This would not end until one side was completely wiped out.

Just as I picked up a spear, I heard children. They were screaming. The little ones had been trapped inside a burning building. The homes would burn in very little time. I had to hurry.

I am their shaman.

I rushed into my home, which was already starting to catch fire and grabbed my staff as well as a raccoon skull.

Teacher, guide me.

There was only one way to put the flames to rest. I had to call the rain, and with Eoha possessed, I had to perform the *shiriwen hokki marapto* ceremony alone. I prayed to the goddess of fire, the *kamui* of the river and springs. While praying to a raccoon skull, I thought of Moyuk village.

I never should have left.

143

I prayed more as I offered libations to the skull and dripped water over myself. Despite all my efforts it did not rain.

Was the great kamui taking the sides of our attackers? No. Impossible. The dreaded Nitne Kamui must have deceived the kamui into going against the chief kamui himself. The Dark One is winning the heavenly war.

"Take this!" The leader of the bear hunt tossed me a spear. I grabbed it and pierced it through a woman who was coming at me with a sharpened stick.

She was dead. I killed her.

I had to keep killing to survive. The women came after me, one of them firing an arrow into my side.

Eoha came into view, spears and arrows in his back.

It didn't seem real.

He moved as if he wasn't injured. The wounds were deep. I had to help him.

I rushed to him, almost getting speared by him once I got too close. "It's me, your little flower bud." I was breaking down into tears.

He charged into more enemies.

Three men came at me at once. I parried the first strike, but the second pierced my arm. My spear was pulled from my grip, and I was pinned down before I could grab any arrows.

Whack!

My head exploded with pain and I fell unconscious.

I awoke, breathing intensely.

Was it all a dream?

The *chisei* I was in…it didn't feel like home.

A figure entered.

Horokeu.

I pushed my back against the wall and looked for some kind of weapon.

"The battle is over." He smiled at me.

"Eoha. Where is he?" I asked, my body trembling.

"Your people brought this on themselves, you know. The Isepo came to us, seeking to unite all the tribes. We despised your people, but the Isepo were very convincing. We set up peace negotiations to be held after the bear feast."

"And that's when you poisoned our shaman."

"Wrong. It was one of your own who did it. They didn't want peace between the tribes. They wanted war."

Brother wouldn't do that. Not ever.

"You have no proof. He had no motive."

"You know him well. He would not accept peace. I didn't want it either. Besides, with the shaman dead, your village would have to welcome you back. His hatred of us and love of you brought him to kill one of his own. And it ended up with your people destroyed."

It all makes sense. Why does it make sense?

"You used poison. You must have."

"The Horokeu are proud warriors. Our two tribes have fought for many generations. We never once used poison against your people."

"That's a lie! Father was killed by a poison arrow."

"Your father was killed by an arrow, but it wasn't poisoned."

"How would you know?"

"I was the one who fought him."

I rushed at the man, digging my nails into his throat before he pressed me to the ground. "Be careful. If you act out, the captive people of your tribe will be put to rest."

I stared at him defiantly. "Your people enslaved us. That was the outcome you wanted, isn't it?"

"After the Isepo chief was murdered, we tried to convince the Isepo to wipe you out. They refused. Instead they decided that we each take a portion of your crops. If we kept you suppressed, there would be no need for your annihilation. But your people spit at our offer and killed both of our chiefs."

Is this how the world is. One is seen as evil and the other as good. Eoha was right. There is no good and no evil. Eoha! He has to be alive.

"Tell me! Where is he?" I broke down into tears.

The man had the audacity to place his hand on my shoulder. "The women and children who survived are working in our gardens." His honeyed voice twisted my stomach. "The men of your village have all gone away."

Gone.

I didn't cry. I couldn't. Emptiness took over me. I could not will myself to move.

"You should be grateful. I won't make you slave away in the fields. You can't be a shaman anymore, but you will be my wife." He leaned down and grabbed my face.

Nothing feels real anymore.

Days went by, all meaningless. With Eoha gone, I decided to go into mourning. When my captor was away on a journey, I shaved my head with a sharpened shell.

The pain was welcoming. It was my punishment for cursing my people.

The Shitumbe were no more. All my fault.

When my captor returned, he found me in a widow's bonnet and dressed in black.

He sat down and cleaned the cuts on my head.

I hope my curse takes his life.

I sat in silence.

After three days of silence, he brought me teacher's staff.

I tossed it into the hearth and watched it burn.

Never again will I speak to the gods. Even the goddess of fire had betrayed me.

My captor took me out for a celebration feast once the memorial rituals were over.

I zoned in and out of consciousness periodically.

A young woman tried to speak to me, but I heard nothing.

Time lost its hold over me.

My captor dressed me up for the coming bear festival. There were Horokeu and Isepo attendees, as well as *ainu* whose garments I was unfamiliar with. I turned away once the bear cub was brought out.

I can't watch him die.

In a daze I stood up and placed my body over the bear cub.

Please, let me just save one life.

My captor lifted me up and pulled me aside.

"If you stop it, if you save him, I'll do anything for you," I said in tears.

He approached the chief and spoke on my behalf.

It was all for naught.

The little bear screamed as he died.

In the end I was unable to change anything. It was all meaningless.

That night my captor took me out to the lake. His words did not reach me.

Nothing did.

He cooked and we ate together. He complimented me and slowly undressed me. His fingers felt cold as they touched me.

Eoha, I miss you.

I pulled back and cried.

I slept alone that night.

One day there was great panic. The sun had been swallowed up by the moon.

Men and women both were screaming "The luminary is dying!" "The sun is dying!"

This was it, a total eclipse. The end of all life.

My dreams of complete darkness may have been premonitions after all.

At this point, I welcomed the darkness to come. I wanted it to swallow up the whole world.

Men tossed *aka* in the air, pleading "*Kamui atemka.*" "*Kamui atemka.*"

They were powerless in reviving the sun god.

I will end it myself. The longer I postpone my destiny, the greater the pain it will bring.

I walked out of the village and ventured into the forest. I found a cliff and dropped down.

The kamui can no longer control me. I'm free.

The entire world was consumed in darkness.

PART 3: ANGEL'S APOTHEOSIS

Chapter 9: The Mirror World

Total darkness. I awoke in a daze.

Am I alive?

In front of me was a tunnel. I went into it, not sure what lay beyond.

I soon realized where I was. This place was the *Pokna Moshiri*, the intermediary zone where spirits can mingle. I noticed some familiar spirits as I journeyed deeper.

No point in staying. They will just be taken from me once again.

I walked past friends, family, and even Eoha, following the light until arriving at a three-way fork in the path.

One road led to the *Kamui Moshiri*, one led to the underworld, and the other would bring me back home to *Kannaa Moshiri*.

Eyes glowed in the dark.

If I tried to take the wrong path, they would surely catch me.

I didn't feel like going anywhere. I didn't want another chance at life. Only misery would await me. I wasn't worthy of going to *Kamui Moshiri*, but I didn't desire punishment either. Maybe just staying in this intermediary zone would be best. Here I could fade away, along with all my misfortune.

Broken and forgotten, just like my people.

Flames erupted and took the form of the fire goddess. Her glory was beyond comprehension, just as she shifted into something recognizable, she turned into something else.

"Do you deny the violence you committed? If you do, I will conjure up your entire life, every violent word and action."

But not my thoughts. Not even the gods can see into our minds.

"I let my desire for revenge and my sense of hopelessness erode my morals. I killed man and animal unnecessarily. I am fully aware of what I have done. I ask for no mercy. Do as you see fit," I said, lowering my head.

"For your transgressions, you belong in *Teinei-Pokna-Shiri*. However, your honesty is worth considering, and you yourself were deceived. Go to *Kamui Moshiri*. Leave now before I change my mind."

I followed the path, guided by guardian *kamui*, until the light got brighter and brighter.

At one point I must have lost consciousness.

I awoke in a white grass bed.

Is this it?

It was different than I expected. The grass was white, or maybe I just perceived it as white.

I wandered around the area for what felt like days before discovering a small community.

They were all Ainu. I recognized some of the people from my own village, others were Isepo, and the dreaded Horokeu were there as well, along with some other tribes.

What happened? Did they give up on their tribal rivalry once they died? After what happened to the Shitumbe, how could any of them live alongside Horokeu?

I have to find out what's going on.

I went into one of the huts.

"Who are you?" asked a young girl.

"How long have you lived here?" I asked.

"I don't know. The sun never goes down," she said.

"Do you know someone called Eoha?"

The girl shook her head.

"You died, right?"

She nodded.

Everyone here is a spirit. I made it to the mirror world. I have to find Eoha. Then we can remarry and live together for the rest of eternity.

I walked around and asked if anyone had seen Eoha. They had not, and they didn't know where other villages were.

What if he didn't make it? What if he went to the wet underground world? I'm to blame for all his misfortune.

I didn't stay in the village. The sight of all the tribes getting along twisted my stomach. I ventured onward to look for other villages.

Before I could find the next one, a bright pink ball of energy appeared before me.

"Welcome to Lum. I am Evol, the Deity of Love. It is a pleasure to be reacquainted with you," said the floating ball of energy.

I didn't know who or what this was, but I lowered my head in respect. "My name is Ebui. Are you aware of the eclipse? Has all life come to an end in the world of the living?"

"The eclipse has passed. Life is progressing all across the living world. All is well," said Evol.

Then it really wasn't the end of times. Though I suppose it makes no difference. Everyone I cared for is already gone. Wait, they're dead!

"Evol, I'm looking for a young man called Eoha. Is there any way you could locate him for me?"

"You must let such attachments free. As long as you hold memories and desires, your next incarnation will be out of reach."

Another incarnation. Another life of misery and misfortune. I'd be a fool to want that.

"I want to stay here. Eoha is my first spouse; we're supposed to get remarried here. If you don't know where he is, can you lead me to someone who would know?"

"Would you like to know how to reincarnate?" asked Evol.

"I want to leave that world behind. I don't want to be a human again."

"There are many potential incarnations. You could return as a wide variety of animals."

What? That wasn't what I was told.

"I need to speak with your leader. Can you grant me an audience with the *kotan kara kamui*?"

"Lum is beyond us all. I can take you to see another deity."

"That will be fine."

"I'll lead the way."

I followed the chipper *kamui* up to a river.

"Is it going to meet us here?" I asked, staring into the *aka*.

"Surely you understand. The river is the Deity of Fate," said Evol.

Fate.

"This body of water goes across every region of Lum. It shifts the tides of events both in this world and the world of the incarnated."

This kamui was responsible for my misfortune. It brought about the annihilation of my people. Yet I'm powerless to do anything against it.

"Fate says that it has located Eoha. Follow me."

"No."

As long as this god exists, misfortune will cling to me. Joining back with my husband will only bring him strife.

"Leave me be."

"I'm very proud of your decision. When your soul is ready for your next incarnation, I'll send an angel your way," said Evol before vanishing into a door of light.

I was alone and powerless. All I could do was wait until all my memories faded and with them, my identity.

I rested by the river bank, though I found myself unable to sleep.

It was something about the air in this place. It made it difficult to relax.

That night, I heard a voice. It came from the river. "You were destined to go to Sel, but I saw potential in you. The possibility of you going to Lum became a reality."

I leaned over and stared into the body of water. "What do you want from me? Haven't I gone through enough already?"

"You are one who understands destiny. Both Sel and Lum seek to change the balance and shift destiny in their favor. You can save both realms. Speak with the Lum gods on my behalf. But before that, you must become an angel."

"I will decide what I do," I said, staring defiantly at the *kamui*.

"Your destiny is not yet writ. Will you incarnate again?"

"I refuse!"

"Or will you become a mawali and shape the system?"

"What is a mawali?" I asked.

"Mawalis are visitors who have bathed in the Good One's light. They are like angels only they were not born from the union of two angels."

This was my chance. If I joined the gods, I could change the way the entire system works. I might even be able to break man's reliance on the gods.

"What do you stand to gain?" I asked.

"Peace of mind."

I was thrown off. I never expected a god to say something like that. I always believed they sought entertainment, not peace.

I stood up from the ground. "I'm going to help you."

"Together we can save Sellum."

I will change this place and my own world along with it.

Chapter 10: Mawali

As soon as I sought out Evol, the *kamui* appeared.

"Can you read my thoughts?" I asked.

"I felt your desire to see me," said the *kamui*.

"I've decided. Make me into an angel," I said, channeling a strength I thought had abandoned me long ago.

"You will make a wondrous addition to the sustainers of Lum," said Evol with a twirl.

This is merely the starting point.

The *kamui* led me to a massive tree. "This is the World Tree. From here the Good One's grace is filtered into this world. Hop on." Evol sprouted wings and had me mount.

The *kamui* rose up the tree.

This tree is taller than any mountain I had ever seen. This world is so different than the stories I was told.

Once we were out of the foliage, I could see the very top.

A waterfall of light was pouring down from a dome partly concealed beyond the clouds. The waterfall broke at the top of the tree and dripped down the sides, revitalizing it with the essence of the gods.

"What will happen to me?" I asked as I was brought closer to the light stream.

"You will be purified and become divine."

And then I will hold sway over the system that traps me and my people. I will change the system that binds all of creation.

I entered the light stream.

No going back now.

Thoughts and memories were buried under an overpowering radiant devotion. But the feeling of my cursed existence and the unjust way of the world was too complex to be taken over.

The light coated my body and erupted out my back as white wings.

I had become a lesser *kamui*.

"Purification successful. You will be assigned a region to overlook by the deity of life."

I jumped off the deity. My wings spread and carried me through the skies.

Freedom.

The wind felt so welcoming. It was as if I could go anywhere. I wanted to keep flying around, but I was focused on my goal.

I landed at the entrance to the World Tree.

Evol appeared and led me inside. "The Deity of Life is responsible for assigning the angels their posts and overseeing their actions."

Even angels are at the whims of the true kamui.

The Deity of Life was something entirely unrecognizable. It was small and clearly not human. The creature's voice echoed in my head. "You will govern the village of humans you first came across. Report to me if they break any commandments."

Just as I was about to ask what the commandments were, I stopped. Somehow I already had knowledge of them.

Evol created a light doorway to the village. We entered and arrived.

Here I am, a guardian kamui over my own tribe and the tribes of my enemies. Is this just another game orchestrated by the chief kamui?

Evol talked to the six chiefs and told them that I would be surveying them. The chiefs reluctantly agreed.

Time was immeasurable here. Still, it felt like a few cycles passed without any problems. Then came the day I found a young man and woman wrapped together. It brought flashes of some experience I had but with whom I had no idea. The couple noticed me and froze up.

They had broken Lum's commandment.

I grabbed the man and separated the two.

"Please, we love each other dearly. Perhaps we can offer you something," said the young woman, folding her hands.

She was of Horokeu and he was Shitumbe.

The two clans should never merge.

I can't explain what came over me, but in a fit of fear and rage I attacked the woman.

The man grabbed onto me, pleading me to stop.

A part of me felt I should report the crime to Efil.

No. I can handle this on my own. Without showing my independence, I will never ascend.

"If I find you two making contact, even if it is merely holding hands, I will dispense justice on you myself."

The moral fabric of this realm was fragile. Firm decisions were needed to keep Lum pure.

159

I left the *chisei.*

It wasn't too long before I found them again.

They looked so happy together.

I disposed of the threat swiftly. One hand pierced through both of their throats. They were dead before they even knew I was there.

Death wasn't supposed to exist in the afterworld. Wait. Of course it does. Why would I think anything to the contrary?

I took the empty husks and tossed them into a gathering of people. "These two were caught trying to usurp the Good One's power. Creation belongs to the gods and the gods alone. The next visitor who defies the Good One will face a more painful end."

My words felt foreign to me. Had I really become so cold?

I felt a sudden calling to return to the World Tree and immediately took flight.

Efil greeted me upon arrival. "Why did you not report the disturbance to me?"

"I was more than capable. I gave a warning. They did not listen."

"Mawali, you cannot allow your own ego to compromise the stability of this realm."

"All I do is for the Good One."

"There is something you should know. Recently, the Good One has sent angels past the realm's border. They have killed demons from the other side. This has caused demons to attack Lum periodically. Balance can only be maintained as long as both sides of Sellum are in harmony. Compromise is our only option."

"I have my duty, but I will choose how I carry it out."

Even when fated, we can always choose how to confront that fate.

"The Good One has asked me to send you past the border. You will be grouped with a squad of angels and mawali."

I bowed.

I'm moving further up the ranks already.

Four mawali—myself and three humanoids—two fox angels as sub-commanders, and a wolf as commander made up the attack squad.

There is something about the commander that irks me.

Our mission was to cross the border into the other side of Sellum and covertly kill off a charismatic demon lord.

The mawalis, myself included, were suited up in armor, though not the fortified armor that the true angels were clad in.

Fear overcame me once we reached the border.

The other side of Sellum, the dark side, was charred and foreboding. Rather than trees, there were metal sculptures popping out of the land. The surface of the ground was made of animals, all human. They were still alive.

What kind of world is this?

The despair in their eyes pierced through my armor. I looked away.

We stood just at the border, letting the soot cling to our armor till it no longer shined.

"Conceal your wings. Follow me," said the wolf angel, rushing ahead.

"Is this your first time crossing? It's mine," said a male human mawali.

"It is," I said, hesitation clinging to my voice like the soot around me.

Our squad, Purity's Warriors, successfully infiltrated a village of demons.

Such hideous creatures. No wonder the Good One wants them removed.

The demon lord, our target, was speaking to a crowd. He was keeping them all focused on him and not on us.

"We must retreat," said the wolf.

One of the demons had spotted our fox angel and was coming to investigate.

The wolf angel emitted a blast of light. Together we rushed out of the village and to the other side of the border.

"We cannot complete the mission as we are now," said the wolf commander.

"We can try again later," I said.

"The peace we have with the other side is fragile. I shall discuss with the other commanders to form a new strategy." The commander left us.

I returned to my post at the tribal village. After following one of the men as he discretely left the village, I saw him grab a weapon beneath the grass. He may have noticed me because he took a moment before initializing his plan.

He invited one of the men to go hunting with him. The two of them set off when I turned the corner, not knowing I would immediately turn around.

They entered the woods and came across a bear.

As one man raised his bow at the bear, the other raised it at the man.

I have to act quickly.

I dropped down from the trees, shot in place of the bear. The other arrow pierced my attacker. As the bear hunter bled out, the human hunter fled.

I took flight and dive-bombed into him, causing us both to tumble down the hillside.

The man's face lit up upon seeing me. He embraced me. "*Mataki.*"

I pushed him off.

Why does he feel so familiar?

"Why were you hunting?" I asked.

"That man was Horokeu; they may live with our people in this place, but they cannot be trusted. They killed you too, didn't they?"

How did I die?

"My past life is not your concern. Why should I not kill you?"

"Sister, what happened to you? How did you die?"

"I don't know who you are. And it doesn't matter how I died. I live for the Good One."

"Has becoming an angel made you forget who you are? I am Akno, and you are Ebuike. We are Shitumbe at heart." The young man lifted his shirt, revealing a fox carving on his chest.

This was not mere trickery. This human knew me. And that symbol means something to me. He looked so familiar.

He was older than me and taller too. With his muscular build, hunting bow and war club, he looked rather capable in battle. His messy hair separated him from some of the more well-groomed humans. Whenever they looked at me, his eyes would sparkle. He was both foreign and familiar all at once.

"If I catch you hunting again, you will join the others who defy the Good One."

"I invite the Horokeu men to hunt with me and then I kill them. If they were willing to break the commandments of Lum by killing a fellow visitor, do they not deserve death?"

"You are not an angel. Such action is not permitted. Only those worthy of upholding Lum's commandments have the authority to punish those who defy them."

"I understand. I shall never fire another arrow. But if I can get them to agree to go hunting…if I lead them out here, will you kill them?"

The hope in his eyes made me feel warm.

"Why not become an angel? You feel very strongly about Lum's commandments," I said, grabbing his hand.

"There are things I refuse to forget. So, shall we work together?"

"Those who would succumb to temptation are just as guilty as those who sin without provocation. We shall purify this village of all those who defy the Good One."

"I shall signal you when I find another sinner," said Akno.

Images from my previous life would flash for an instant before being buried under devotion. I was once a mother, a warrior, and even a lover. It all seemed to be from the same life, but I had no way of knowing for sure. It wasn't too long before the wolf commander approached me.

It was time to try again.

"Come with me." The wolf led us into a cave.

"Why are we hiding?" asked the male human mawali.

"Only humanoid angels can infiltrate the other side. But you will need a disguise first." The wolf suddenly jumped the human man.

Before I could react, one of the foxes was on top of me, clawing and biting at my flesh.

I didn't struggle like the others. It was obvious that this was done so that we would look like demons.

The foxes sewed up our wounds with metal string.

An already injured human mawali entered the cave with a torch.

The others struggled and tried to flee. I stepped up to go first.

With our flesh charred, our skin sewed up and our bodies beaten, we were ready to fulfill the Good One's task.

With each successful mission I will gain credibility. That credibility shall bring about my ascension all the way to the top.

Chapter 11: Ascension

We successfully infiltrated the demon lord's rally.

"They should really treat us better. Without humans in Lum, this operation would be impossible," said the male mawali.

"You don't think they allow humans to become angels just because we look like demons, do you?" asked the woman human mawali.

"Destiny has brought us here. Now, let's complete our mission and get out of here," I said, gradually moving closer to the stage.

Our target was a demon lord from the envy region. He had grafted angel wings onto his back and was dressed in white.

Strange behavior for a demon.

"Did you hear what he said?" asked the male human mawali.

"Balance can only be maintained through compromise. We cannot allow hate to tempt us into war with the angels. Lum and Sel are two sides of the same realm. Though different, they are not antithetical. Both serve a purpose."

The demon lord spoke of peace, not war with the angels.

None of this makes sense.

"Are you sure this is the right one?" asked the male human mawali.

"Absolutely," replied our human commander.

"Shouldn't we be going after the warmongers?"

"We have a mission to uphold."

"I don't understand," said the human female mawali.

166

"Peace is not an option. Demons by their very existence threaten the stability of Lum. As mawali, it is our duty to fulfill Lum's mission," said the commander.

"I understand," I said softly.

Good and evil were fighting for supremacy. It all felt so familiar. But why would the good desire war?

"We move in all at once," said the commander, forming a light spear.

I nodded.

All four of us rushed the stage.

We fired beams of light to blind both the crowd and the guards on stage.

By the time the demon lord's body hit the floor, we were already at the exit.

Panic caused the demons to disperse, masking our escape all the way to the edge of the village.

"We should be working with demons like that, not fighting them," said the male human mawali before a spear pierced his throat.

I took a step back, watching our commander to decipher his next attack.

"Why did you kill him!?" screamed the female human mawali.

"Fresh mawalis were chosen for this job specifically because it was controversial. The Good One left me in charge of keeping things under wraps. She doesn't trust mawali," he said, tearing out the spear and turning his sights on the woman.

I stepped up to him. "What kind of god lives in fear?" I gripped the spear, tore it from his grip, and beheaded him. I dropped the weapon and approached my fellow mawali. "We should report back. The captain died during the mission, agreed?"

She nodded, still fear-stricken.

"Are you coming?" I asked.

"If we go back, they'll kill us. We're already in disguise. We should stay in Sel, where humans are welcome."

"If that's where you feel you belong, then go," I said before walking off.

When I met up with the angels in the cave, I reported that the mission was completed, but I was the only one left. To fill the void in the chain of command, and because of my skills, I was promoted to the rank of captain. I did some reconnaissance missions with a new group of mawali who looked up to me and put their faith in my leadership. When I wasn't doing recon, I was killing sinners alongside my human ally. Eventually I was assigned to negotiate with Absence: the realm between realms. On my own, I went to the rendezvous point and met a rather peculiar character.

"Ah, you must be the one I've been looking for," he said, staring into me.

The emissary of Absence was a crystalline man wrapped in a clear robe.

"Have you been waiting long?" I asked, bowing in apology.

"We are kindred spirits. We both seek change beyond our abilities," he said, stepping up to me.

How does he know so much about me?

"Are you going to take me to Absence?"

"In a moment, yes. Tell me, what is it you seek?"

"All I do is for the glory of the Good One."

"Ah, yes, of course." He created a portal and walked in with me.

We arrived in a land of nothingness. There was no earth or sky.

"The Good One has proven to be a useful ally."

"What is it you seek?" I asked before suddenly dreading the possible answer he may give.

"Freedom, just like you. There are obstacles in our way. Etaf is determined to keep things as they are. I would prefer you as the Deity of Fate."

How did he know what I sought? Had someone told him? No. I'm the only one who knows that. He's dangerous.

"You needn't be afraid. The system of Sellum has grown stale. Even when flooded by Lum's light, you can see that. But if you were to become a goddess, I could dispel that light from you," he said, touching my wings.

"What do you want in return?" I asked, looking at him with all the strength I could muster.

"We both want the same thing. You owe me nothing. Now, shall we get on with this charade?" he asked, leading me into another portal.

After the peace meeting, which proceeded smoothly, I was escorted back to Lum.

"How can I become Etaf?" I asked.

"I'll put in a good word for you. The Good One favors me and my advice."

Things proceeded as normal, with peace meetings in Absence, sabotage in Sel, and cleansing in Lum. After killing three sinners at once with my human ally, the emissary of Absence appeared.

"Who is he?" asked Akno, standing in front of me in a protective stance.

"I am Crystal, guard and emissary of Absence. How did someone like you make it to Lum?" he asked, peering beyond Akno's flesh.

"What is that supposed to mean?"

"Of course. Vengeful, violent and war hungry—you were chosen for your vices not your virtues. The Good One should be more particular about who she lets in."

I approached the emissary. "Why have you come to this village?"

"I came to forward the Good One's message. By reasons beyond my understanding, Etaf is no more. The river exists and still flows all across Lum, but it's as if the deity's individuality was fragmented and could not be sustained. Naturally the deity's powers have returned to the Good One."

"Absurd, *kamui* can't die," said Akno.

"Death isn't what I would call it. Either way, you must meet with the Good One. She has chosen you to be the next Etaf. You will represent more than the Good One, you will represent all mawali and every human in Lum. Whether she chose you for political reasons or due to your qualifications, your actions have enough weight to bring either peace or war."

Every word he spoke felt like it had a hidden meaning. Nothing he said could be trusted. Even so, I couldn't have gotten this far without his help.

Akno put his arms around me. "You've broken age-old traditions once more. I couldn't be more proud of my little sister," he said, beaming at me.

"Thanks." I hugged him back.

He felt so warm and welcoming. It was like I was home again.

"Come with me," said Crystal, bringing me into the forest to meet with Evol.

The Deity of Love congratulated me and created a portal.

I went inside and arrived in a place hidden behind the clouds. It was a castle of light.

"Your loyalty has not gone unnoticed. Neither have your appointments with that human," said the Good One, her voice emanating from the floor, walls, and ceiling all at once.

"His actions only serve to uphold the peace and stability of your realm," I said.

"You care for him deeply, don't you?" asked the voice, each word echoing in my mind.

"He knows the me that I've forgotten."

"Some things are best forgotten. You are soon to be a goddess. I don't want you meeting with him anymore. Is that understood?"

"As you command," I said with a bow.

"You will obey my every whim. My words are that of the realm itself," said the Good One.

"You are absolute," I said, bowing with reverence.

"If you betray me, human, you will be disposed of. This is the only chance your kind will ever get. You are now the Goddess of Fate," said the Good One.

Light energy came out from the walls and pooled into me. It wasn't like the concentrated light from the waterfall; it was far more powerful. It revitalized my body without affecting my mind.

"The merge was successful. Return to me once you've had a vision. I must know what the future holds for my realm. Evol shall be by your side as an interpreter. I'm not foolish enough to trust your word. Now, be off," said the Good One.

I formed a portal and arrived just outside the village I was once charged with monitoring.

Crystal rose out from the lake that was once a deity. "Ah, rather refreshing, isn't it? I see you've been promoted. Many congratulations," he said, clapping his hands slowly.

"What happens next?"

"There's been rumor of a promiscuous mawali who has transcended the species boundary. I am rather interested—"

"I mean with me," I said, gazing at him in hopes of uncovering his plan.

"You're right where you need to be. Once I've returned your memories, we needn't meet again."

"I don't want that. I've grown stronger without my memories."

"Then I wish you luck in all your future endeavors." He walked off into the forest.

I doubt that's the last I'll see of him.

My duty as the Goddess of Fate was enjoyable. Evol would interpret the overall vibe of my erratic dancing, but the deity was unable to fathom negative concepts so I always had to re-decipher its interpretation. There were prophecies as simple as the ascension of a new mawali, but there were also visions that led to the discovery of rebel spies in the angelic infantry. One particularly peculiar prophecy was about the ascension of a deity. The Good One at first interpreted this as a potential threat to her throne. I felt my interpretation, that the alleged "ascension" would be more accurately understood as "death," made more sense. Each subsequent premonition led to another piece of information, until it was readily apparent that the Deity of Life, who had existed in Lum even before the Good One herself, was to die by my hand. Finding this prophecy problematic, Lum sent me to Sel on a mission to retrieve a god who was assumed either captured or dead. If I returned without the god, the Good One threatened to purge the village I once kept watch over.

At the edge of the realm, I found myself face-to-face with the emissary from Absence yet again.

"It's a bit worrisome that the Good One is sending you without informing the other gods."

I channeled my aura into a sword and raised it. "Was it you who put that vision in my head?"

"Pardon?" he asked so authentically it was suspicious.

"My power is to create crystals, nothing more, nothing less," he said.

"Then how were you going to bring back my memories?"

"I was going to propose you allow the River of Fate to cleanse you of Lum's light, but you decided not to. Have I ever given you a reason to doubt my intentions?" asked the emissary.

"I have a mission to fulfill," I said, walking past the border and into Sel.

"Ah, but if you truly wanted to follow the Good One's wishes, you would not complete it. Having a mawali, and a human at that, go traitor would fit her agenda nicely."

"Is that what you're after as well?"

"That has yet to be determined. If you do return, things will no doubt change."

"I will return, and I will bring glory to the Good One."

"Your loyalty is superficial; you wear it as armor. Before I go, here's something for you to ponder. Once the war is over, what will happen to the humans? And what use are mawali in times of peace?" asked Crystal before vanishing.

More tricks and deception. I will not give his paranoia the attention he desires.

I entered Sel, but with my divine aura it was impossible to blend in. Not that I needed to. No mere demon could stand against me or the Destiny Sword. I must have killed hundreds of them. The longer I spent in this place, the less devotion I held toward the Good One. It was as if my faith was being sapped by the energy of the realm and slowly filled in with doubt.

What if the Good One sent me here to kill demons? Perhaps she doesn't want to paint me as a traitor after all. It seems even more likely she is using me to inspire mawali and humans to seek war with the demons. I'm a scapegoat for her war propaganda, and since she banished me, the Good One need not take responsibility for my actions.

Unable to vanquish me, the Dark One sent an emissary to bargain with me. The emissary was clad in golden armor formed by his shimmering aura. He was clearly no demon.

"I am Egaruoc. Were you banished, or did you come here of your own volition?" he asked.

"I am Etaf. I was sent on a mission to retrieve you. I didn't expect you to come to me. Tell me, have you allied with these demons?" I asked, ready to draw out my sword at a moment's notice.

"It takes bravery to go into battle against a powerful enemy. But it takes true courage to see things from your enemy's perspective, reevaluate your position, and fight for an end to the hostility. I ask that you join me in my quest to unify Sellum once more."

"Once more? You think Sel and Lum were once at peace?"

"They were indeed. Before the second wave of realm gods took over, the realms had no conflict. The concept of good and evil is what has brought about the turmoil between them. And it is that very concept that I have sworn to oppose."

Good and evil are universal truths. They can't be mere constructs…can they?

"Come with me."

The God of Courage led me to the demon graveyard. It was several acres long and had small tombstones that paid tribute to the demons killed by Lum's forces.

"I'm partly responsible," I said, turning away as I noticed a loved one praying to their dearly departed.

Egaruoc placed his hand on my shoulder. "As am I. We are gods, Etaf. We have the power to make a difference for angels and demons."

I drew my sword. "There is someone I wish to see again. If I don't bring you back, I cannot return. My loyalties lie with Lum above all else."

"Giving away your freewill won't protect you from sorrow. Letting someone else command you does not rid you of the responsibilities you have for your actions. This is your chance to join with me to bring back the balance."

His words remind me of Crystal's. Has he been compromised by that dubious emissary?

"Good and evil may be mere concepts, and I may be acting selfishly, but I will bring you back. Draw your weapon," I said, summoning up the Destiny Sword.

"If either side is annihilated, then both sides lose. There is no victory in war."

I thrust my sword at him.

"*Courage.*"

Golden chains wrapped around my blade.

"I was the commander of Lum's forces before I was captured. You will not defeat me."

"My destiny is to return. No amount of skill or cunning can change that." I jumped back and cut the air.

"***Valor***."

A shield of golden light appeared in front of Egaruoc, but my slice passed right through it.

"All things collapse when faced with their destiny. ***Spatial Slice***."

Another cut and I had him on his knees.

"Enough. I concede. I'll come along with you. Please, allow me to say goodbye to my beloved. I do not know if she and I will ever meet again."

"Love is something that must be abandoned if we seek equality."

"Love is the fuel to my rebellious spirit," he said, standing up.

His wounds had already healed.

I raised my sword.

"Make the portal. I'll come along," he said, raising his hand.

I formed the portal and made sure he went through first.

"I have returned, along with the Lum god. My mission is completed. Have I proven my loyalty?"

A portal appeared and the Deity of Life emerged.

"Is the Good One pleased with me?" I asked.

"Egaruoc has been in Sel far too long. He has been compromised. Kill him and the Good One will welcome you back."

"I seek peace, not war," said Egaruoc.

"I am a mere servant to the Good One. I do not judge your actions. That said, I cannot defy the Good One's wishes," said Efil.

"What you can't defy is fate. I will not kill him, but if you attack, I will kill you," I said with firm intensity.

"You cannot sway me," said Efil.

"You will die, Efil. And it will be by my blade. It has already been predetermined. Are you certain you wish to bring that destiny into the present moment?"

"You cannot kill life itself, but all it takes to kill courage is the certainty of death." Efil released its aura, transforming the landscape into a jungle instantaneously.

"I cannot die yet. My union with my beloved shall bring both the realms back together! *Bravery*!" exclaimed Egaruoc, layering strands of his aura into a sword. "With Bravery in hand, I will fight!"

"I have never once been in battle," said Efil, swerving out of the way of each slash.

"Defend yourself, Egaruoc. I must be the one to strike down the deity!" I exclaimed before slashing the air.

"*Life*." Efil aged a tree next to me, causing it to topple over.

As I took a step forward to slash once more, the ground beneath me crumbled.

My slashes passed through Efil.

How is that possible?

"I have control over the aging process. Your aura can only target the living."

"Wait? He died to dodge your attack? We cannot win the battle. We must run," said Egaruoc.

"You can't run," said Efil, condensing its aura.

Egaruoc dodged and his sword fired chains at the deity.

"One day even time will cease to exist," said Efil.

The jungle around us died and regenerated. Efil used the reanimated trees as cover and fired its aura out as a beam at us.

Egaruoc pushed me aside and created a shield with his aura.

The shield dissolved.

"Stop hiding! Fight me face to face!" yelled Egaruoc, dodging the incoming blasts.

The ground beneath us fell apart.

Egaruoc solidified his aura beneath him and grabbed hold of me.

"I am every creature that will ever take form. *Adaptation*." Efil's aura burst out, forming muscles, scales, and feathers around it.

The once tiny deity had become larger than a bear.

"You need not kill the deity. We need to make it back to Sel, that's all," said Egaruoc, forming a portal.

"*Life*."

Energy burst out from the ground, aging the portal into oblivion.

Scales fired off from Efil and pierced into me. The deity then slammed into me, gripped me in its talons, and took flight.

"*Courage!*" Egaruoc fired his strands of energy at the deity, piercing its wings. "My will can surpass any obstacle!" he yelled, running up his own energy strands toward the deity.

The deity shed its feathers. The feathers turned into a torrent of birds that sped into Egaruoc.

The God of Courage stacked multiple shields with his golden aura as he rushed to the Deity. Once close enough, he fired out chains of courage.

Glyphs of energy formed around the deity. Its skin then emitted seeds which grew into airborne trees that deflected the chains. The deity's aura then erupted out from the tip of the trees and crashed into Egaruoc.

This time fate is mine to command.

I closed my eyes, focused my aura into the Destiny Sword, and plunged it into Efil. "*Doom.*"

My aura flooded the deity from within. The deity burst, its flesh decaying before touching the ground.

"Blind loyalty brings only sorrow," said Egaruoc, grabbing me in midair.

"How did you survive that?" I asked.

"A brave spirit keeps you young I've been told." Egaruoc flew toward land and set me on the ground by a lake. "It seems even gods can age."

My body was no longer that of a teenage girl. Efil's aura must have hit me when the deity burst. I had developed into a woman in an instant.

"Let us return to Sel…where we can work toward peace. There is no negotiating with one who believes she is all that is good," said Egaruoc.

"Go on without me." I wiped away my tears.

"Were you close?"

"No. It's not that."

Even as a god, I cannot escape destiny. After becoming fate itself, I thought things would change.

"Leave. I will not be returning to Sel," I said.

"Etaf, you have more power than you realize," said Egaruoc, before leaving.

The Good One sent angels to attack my village. Rather than fight against them in futility, I joined them in the purging. I made sure their deaths were swift and decisive. Akno had a look of confusion as my spear pierced his heart.

Flashes of another life suddenly came up.

Had I killed him before?

The Good One was impressed with my performance and decided to put me in charge of punishing those who tried to procreate. It was strange, I felt a bit of satisfaction when ending the lives of the pregnant women.

Why should they be entitled to happiness?

Surrendering my will gave me a sense of freedom. Rather than fighting destiny, I moved along with it. Perhaps that was what my duty as Etaf truly was. The more premonitions I had, the more I realized that war was coming. I was given my own battalion to train. I raised the angelic warriors with my philosophy: there is no good or evil. This allowed them to kill without hesitation. Soon they became the most feared angels in Lum.

One day, I had a vision. When Evol spoke the meaning of my divination, I was at a loss for words. "Etaf will either kill Efil or die by her hands."

There wasn't a new God of Life appointed yet, so the prophecy made no sense. Had I misinterpreted before? Was this new Efil the one I was destined to kill and not the old one? The strangest thing about this prophecy was that it gave me a choice: to either kill or die. Egaruoc's words gained new meaning. I did have the power to choose, but yet, not even as the Goddess of Fate could I determine where that choice would lead. Even so, being able to choose empowered me. I was determined to work alongside the new Efil and make her either a worthy enemy to kill or a worthy friend to be killed by.

Find out what happens when this cursed Goddess encounters a new form of life in **Resurrection of The Exps: The Hero of Sel**
AVAILABLE NOW!

https://www.amazon.com/Hero-Sel-Resurrection-Exps/dp/1943733031/ref=sr_1_1?keywords=Resurrection+of+the+Exps%3A+the+hero+of+sel&qid=1574289449&s=books&sr=1-1

Hello, mortal. I humbly beseech thee to consider joining our forces!

You can help shape the destiny of many souls by joining the Patreon page. The benefits offered are not to be missed.

https://Patreon.com/sphere_of_compassion

Also, if you enjoyed my story then you should discover the *Of The Exps* series (3 sci-fi/fantasy books are currently available in eBook and print form).

https://amzn.to/2IN29eR

The dark fantasy story of a young angel's journey to reunite with her family may also interest you.

https://amzn.to/2Y39ahZ

And discover new knowledge on the website!

https://sphereofcompassion.com

REBELLION OF THE EXPS

EXPS

BOOK 1

Alexander J. McCarty

Art by: Gabriel McCarty

TRAILER!

Ch 1: Awakening

Exp 8 Trailer

"Freedom is a shackle."

Exp 8 could only faintly hear these words. Nonetheless, they repeated fervently in its mind.

There was no world for Exp 8. It had no identity. All it knew, all it was, were those words: "freedom is a shackle." Despite this, it didn't have a clue what they meant. They were merely noise.

A mechanical sound broke through the mantra as an automatic door opened. Voices could be heard but only as whispers.

Exp 8's nervous system slowly activated, allowing it to feel the gelatinous fluid that encompassed him. Its eyes opened, frightening the people who were gathered around.

"It's waking up! It's finally waking up! Hurry, go inform Devlin," exclaimed a scientist, his hands trembling as he looked up at the creature in the incubator.

Exp 8 was an imposing height of six feet five inches, towering over the other life-forms in the room. The creature's body was clad in blue-tinted, platinum-colored quicksilver armor an inch thick. The sleek armor shielded all but the being's piercing black eyes. Those eyes had a depth as overwhelming as space itself.

Around Exp 8's head was a cybernetic helmet that protected the soft flesh within. Horizontal slits were carved into the center of the two slabs melded along the jawline, forming a mouthpiece. The slabs curved upward above its head, creating long, functionless ears. Protruding from the back of its helmet were metallic tendrils, wispily floating in the gelatinous fluid. Embedded in the crown of the helmet was an empty clear orb.

A motherly light started to bloom inside the orb as the system booted up. Exp 8's metal-plated chest was concave, funneling in like an ant-lion trap. A dimly lit, sky-blue sphere filled the cavity. A five-foot metallic tail was limply swaying in the liquid.

The creature had strong, thick legs. Sharpened metal plates formed three bladed talons on each foot and one blade in the back for support. Energy gathered in the orbs embedded into the being's large hands. The being's trembling fingers tensed up into fists.

Exp 8's head turned slowly, examining the immediate surroundings. The new life-form deduced that it was floating inside a large shell.

A mere moment ago, Exp 8 would have been unable to understand the concept of *shell*. But for some unfathomable reason, its meaning was clear. Now the creature understood what a shell was and simultaneously felt the desire to escape from it. The reason for wanting to escape had yet to be formulated.

Exp 8 reached out, bumping its hand against the glass.

The creature was imprisoned in a clear incubator filled to the top with a light green liquid.

Exp 8 felt a strange sense of fellowship with this liquid. Both of them were seemingly trapped by nothing.

A large number "8" was painted across the incubator's surface.

Exp 8 dragged its fingers across the number, following its curves. It soon became entranced in the act. The creature felt something both real and fanciful as its fingers made loops around the image. This symbol was somehow a part of the curious life form.

Exp 8 Trailer

Exp 8's arm moved instinctively, breaking free of the trance. Struggling to move the rest of its body, the creature realized multiple tubes and wires had penetrated through its armor and were embedded deep into its flesh.

Now that Exp 8 was aware of their existence, the creature felt pain. It didn't fully grasp the concept, but it was certainly not fond of this new sensation.

Curling up, Exp 8 loosened the pull on its body. Pain still lingering in its eyes, it looked beyond the encasing and into the world outside its little eggshell.

Everything was gray, structured, and lifeless.

It looked beyond the immediate surroundings, peering through the wall and into a hidden room.

Exp 8 was not alone.

Inside the metal room were multiple incubation chambers. Inside each was a life-form, curled up like a fetus. Some of them were missing limbs and others had holes in their bodies. One was belly up, its eyes glazed over.

Exp 8 watched their lifeless bodies attentively and waved its hand, willing them to awaken.

They remained motionless.

Fear of death struck Exp 8 even before the being could fathom its meaning.

Exp 8 saw the shell in a new light. The desire to escape was now wrapped in a layer of fear. The being pushed its trembling hands against the encasing. This world was no longer a shell; it was a cage. The word *cage* brought up the all-too-familiar word *shackle*.

Exp 8 feared that it would die shackled inside its prison. It tried to thrash around but was only able to flail its arms. The creature's head moved the slightest bit forward, but it was unable to reach the encasing. In Exp 8's peripheral vision, something caught its attention.

Beyond the encasing was a group of strange creatures. These life-forms had no prison and were gawking at it with wide eyes.

Exp 8 did not feel threatened by these creatures. The being knew intuitively that, if it escaped, they would be unable to stop it.

The foreign creatures continued to stare, none of them uttering a word.

Exp 8 was befuddled by their astonishment. How could its imprisonment be more astounding to them than their own freedom?

Freedom! The word trapped Exp 8 in a torrent of desire. It did not matter what preceded it. Freedom was now its goal. And escaping from this prison was its only means of attaining it.

The scientists approached closer, their eyes filled with admiration.

Exp 8 peered down at them. They appeared to have skin outside rather than within. Their external material appeared to be more malleable than its own armor and looked completely functionless for self-defense. One creature looked at a metal device on its arm and smiled. Suddenly the lab's twin iron doors flew open, releasing a puff of steam.

"Devlin!" they exclaimed, shaking with excitement and apprehension.

The steam dispersed, revealing a proud grin. Devlin was a loose-bodied youth with a piercing golden right eye. A clump of jet-black hair covered his left eye. He wore a black, unbuttoned lab coat with a cloak that draped over his arms like wings. Beneath the glossy coat was a spiffy blood-red undershirt. From the neck down, he was shielded by a black skintight bodysuit.

Devlin stepped out of the foot-high layer of steam. His feet were comfortably situated in custom-designed metallic boots that gleamed black with a bright red trim. Wrapped around his throat was a necklace with a metal double helix pendant.

Exp 8 could not fathom the idea of arrogance, but Devlin's smile perturbed the creature. It did not seem genuine.

"My creation has finally awoken!" exclaimed Devlin in a dramatic, youthful voice.

The men in the room bashed their hands together gratuitously and smiled as if they relished it.

The notion of these creatures enjoying pain disturbed Exp 8. The creation feared not knowing what these life-forms were capable of.

Devlin looked down at his kin. A cruel smile spread across his face as he opened his lips to speak. "Enough! Enough applause. We can celebrate my success later. Leave us! I wish to speak with Exp 8 alone," he whispered in a harsh, commanding tone.

"Congratulations!" they exclaimed, striking Devlin's shoulder as they left.

The doors shut automatically.

Exp 8 was all alone with Devlin.

TO BE CONTINUED IN EXP 8: REBELLION OF THE EXPS

NOW AVAILABLE IN EBOOK AND PRINT FORMATS.

SEARCH EXP 8 book @ amazon.com

Also, keep an eye out for the **Comic** in 2020.

ISBN 978-1-9437-3302-6

Published by Sphere of Compassion, Inc.

Cover design by Gabriel McCarty

RESURRECTION OF THE EXPS

BOOK 2

THE HERO OF SEL

Alexander J. McCarty
Art by: Gabriel McCarty

TRAILER!

The Crimson Coliseum

The Hero of Sel Trailer

Previously: Exp 8 was knocked out by the Prince of Pleasure's poison. He awoke on the ashy floor of a dark room. "Where the hell am I?" He rattled the searing hot iron bars.

"Calm down. Wait your turn," said a demon.

Exp 8 recognized him.

It was the same crispy demon captain that had led him up the mountain.

"Where is this place?" asked Exp 8, pulling his hands off the bars.

"The center of entertainment, the Crimson Coliseum!" The crispy demon pulled a lever that rose the iron bars up.

"Don't die, alright? You did a good thing in Respite, saving those kids. Beg if you have to. Strike a deal. Don't piss him off," said the charred demon commander.

Exp 8 stepped out of the prison cell and entered the Crimson Coliseum. The structure itself was made from bones, making it more durable than the fleshy buildings he had previously encountered. Tens of thousands of demons were stationed at the pews. Nearly all of them cheered when Exp 8 rose up his fist. There were only a few thousand that raised their fist in solemn silence.

Exp 8 got into a fighting stance as the bars of a nearby cell opened up.

The Baroness of Blades emerged, leaping onto the blood-soaked fleshy arena stage.

Hero of Sel Trailer

"What are you doing…?"

"As Etah's proudest warrior, I will strike you down, hero." She gripped the hilt of one of her rear swords and rushed up to her competitor.

"We can take him on together," said Exp 8, skipping back while using his jets.

"My pride will not allow it. *Ignition!*" The Baroness unsheathed a sword, super heating it in the process. The blade missed Exp 8's head but sliced off one of his tendrils. She swerved out of the way of an orb directed at her face and slammed her bladed foot into her rival.

Exp 8 slid back, directing the momentum to get behind her.

The Baroness grabbed the hilt of a blade at her front and gouged it in.

Exp 8 ducked under her reverse jab and used the opening to stab his talons into her legs.

She ripped the dagger out of her head and jabbed it at his throat, blocked by his arm at each thrust.

Exp 8 gripped the arm holding the dagger and slammed his head into her face. "If this is some kind of ploy, best to end it soon. I don't want to kill you by accident." His turrets rose out from his shoulders.

The Baroness stopped all movement. "I may be incognito, but this fight is real. The winner gets to face Etah. This may be my one chance at taking him down. *Ignition!*" She pulled out a dagger from her knee, set aflame by her boiling blood.

The blade slid up Exp 8's torso and sliced open his shoulder.

Exp 8 gripped onto the blade and twisted the talons he had imbedded in her leg.

The Baroness collapsed to the ground alongside her rival.

Most of the protruding blades slid off Exp 8's armor, but two or three found the gaps and pierced his flesh.

"I don't believe you. You've had plenty of chances to fight Etah." Exp 8 twisted her arm, making her drop the dagger.

"Calling me a coward!" she yelled, biting into his neck.

Exp 8 slammed her against the bloody floor. "You want an audience! You need someone to see your victory. It's not tactics; it's your inflated ego!" He created an orb, gripped it with his gravity field and slammed it into her head repeatedly.

"That's right! Everyone is watching! I won't fail now!" She twisted one of her blades as she tore it out, blinding her rival with a gush of steamy blood.

Only able to see red, Exp 8 felt something slam into his chest. He was rolled onto his back. His vision adjusted through the blood to see a long slab of steel between his fingers. "Make it look good."

The blade slid through his fingers and into his chest.

The Baroness plunged the blade all the way through. "It's over." She stood up, yanked the sword out from his chest and raised it. "I won! I am the greatest warrior."

A few members of the audience cheered. Most were either silent or weeping.

Etah leaped off from his decorated podium.

The impact from his landing splintered the ground.

The God of Hate backhanded the defiant demon lord. "What have you done?"

Hero of Sel Trailer

The Baroness slid back and jabbed a sword into the ground, slowing herself to a halt. "They're all watching. All of them! My pride is at stake!" She rushed at the Deva, wielding two swords in each hand.

"He was supposed to win! To triumph against an unstoppable force! How dare you deny these people their hero!" Etah's aura was sucked into his bulky body. "Death would be mercy. You shall be disgraced!"

The Baroness ducked under his fist and sliced his belly.

Etah's legs slammed into her body like battering rams.

The Baroness jabbed two blades into the Deva's knee and kicked off the ground. She rode the momentum, slicing the god's shoulders and positioning herself behind him.

Etah spun around. "All of it ruined! You want to be a hero so badly! Hmmhmmhmmmhuhuh! The job is yours!" He parried each strike with an equally powerful punch. His foot slammed down on hers, flattening it along with her pride. "Everyone behold! This is the embodiment of your hopes! She alone can save you from your judgment!" The god gripped her swords between two fingers each.

Nearly the whole stadium cheered for their new hero.

"You've taken up their dreams. You've stolen Exp 8's mission by striking him down. Can you live up to their expectations?"

"You will fall with all of Sel watching!" The Baroness dropped the swords and stabbed a dagger into Etah's throat. She twisted it as she ripped out the scorching blade. Lava gushed out of the deity's wound. "Never underestimate me!" she yelled in a frenzy, stabbing his throat with various daggers.

Etah knocked her off.

The Baroness rushed up to the Deva, her hands ready to unsheathe two more swords.

Etah's aura burst out and gripped her hands. His tattoos lit up once she was within range. His hands went around hers. "And so, the rebellion dies!"

"*Ignition!*" The Baroness pulled her blades out halfway before they were pushed completely through her.

Etah twisted the blades and cleaved her body in two.

The Baroness joined the blood-soaked floor.

Moans, screams, and anguish from the pews blotted out all noise.

"This despair, it's superficial. Not nearly enough," said Etah with a clenched fist.

Exp 8 spat out blood.

Etah turned his attention to the fallen hero. His grimace shifted into a wide grin. "Still alive! Heal him!"

Four demons with white wolves and tigers on a leash came out from the sidelines. They went to Exp 8's side and placed their paws on him.

"I'm sorry, I couldn't free you," said Exp 8, tugging at their collar.

White energy poured out from the paws and entered Exp 8.

Within seconds his wounds had closed. Within half a minute, he was glowing with energy.

Etah pulled the leader of the Freedom Forcers off the ground. "Residents of Sel! Your hero has returned from the dead! The battle you came for will now commence!"

The stadium shook, each cheer contributing to the quake of support.

"Come, hero! Fight me here and now in the Crimson Coliseum! End my reign, if you can," said Etah with a beckoning hand.

"No."

Etah took a step forward. "What?"

"I won't move a muscle until you heal her. I know you can do it," said Exp 8, patting his helpers on the head.

"You think a warrior like her would die so easily?" asked Etah, lifting up the demon lord's upper half.

The Baroness ripped out an arrow and jabbed into the tyrant. "Die! Die! I'm not done yet! I won't lose to you!" she yelled, unable to pierce his hardened muscles.

Etah flung her aside.

"Heal her or I'm out."

The God of Hate glared at the defiant hero. "You don't get to command me."

"Have it your way." Exp 8 flew off the ground. He slammed into a thin red aura.

"As if I'd risk letting you leave. Come down here and face me!" yelled Etah.

"Look everyone! See your ruler! Look how he struggles when things don't go as he plans. Marvel at his frustration," said Exp 8, flying circles around Etah.

The deity bit his lip. "Heal her." He turned his head to the demons. "I said heal her!"

The demons dropped their leashes and picked up the Baroness' halves.

"Wait. Stop." Etah looked at the hero and smiled. "I have a better plan. Either fight me...." His red aura shot out like a bullet. It exploded into the crowd like a grenade, killing seven demons immediately and injuring eleven more. "Or I'll dispose of the audience. It's your choice." The merciless tyrant gathered energy in his hand, aiming it at a group of child demons near the front.

Exp 8 sent a volley of orbs at the detestable deity while making circles in the air.

Etah redirected the blast at the Exp, followed by a volley of smaller bursts.

The Ultimate Exp enlarged an orb as he swerved around the attacks, all the while firing at the god's face to disrupt his aiming.

"Your hero will do anything to protect you! Come down, hero, or face the consequences," said Etah, aiming his aura at the audience.

Exp 8 swooped down and slammed into the deity. "I will take you down! BIG BALL SHOT!" He fired off the orb, sending his enemy back a few feet. After reengaging his thrusters, he pummeled Etah's chest, keeping steady fire on the god's face.

"Stop! I'm not done! He's mine!" yelled the Baroness, using her dagger to scale up the arena.

Etah's aura gripped the orb and rammed it into Exp 8. He then grabbed onto the hero's leg.

Exp 8 slammed his talons into the arm holding his leg. He twisted out of the iron grip after firing a pebble-sized orb point blank at the god's face.

"Better hurry," said Etah.

The massive orb from earlier was now heading to a crowd that wasn't dispersing fast enough.

Exp 8 supercharged his jets and slammed his body into the orb, redirecting it to the ground. His jets flipped and backed him out, but he was still caught in the periphery of the blast.

Etah leaped off the ground. His massive hands grabbed onto Exp 8's torso. "You should pay attention."

The hero's jets flipped around again and blasted the god's face.

Exp 8 zoomed by, slicing Etah's back with his elbow talons. "Stop dragging this out. The longer it goes on, the more casualties there will be."

"Hmmhmmhmmmhuhuh. I'm well aware." Etah fired out heated blasts at the hero.

Knowing that a misfire would result in a casualty, Exp 8 slammed into each blast. The freedom fighter then crashed to the ground.

"Even when his life is on the line, the hero defends you! He protects people he has never met! Such valor!" Etah pinned down the mortal with his foot.

"These people aren't strangers. They're enslaved...like I was. We are made kin by our oppression!" Exp 8 struggled beneath the Deva's foot.

"Such powerful words! Though you could have picked a better time for them," said Etah, stepping on the hero's legs with his other foot.

Exp 8 punched the god's foot with great strength but it wouldn't budge. His tail smacked against the God of Hate's leg.

"What was that? Are you mocking me?" asked Etah, glaring down at the nuisance.

"Haven't quite gotten the hang of fighting with my tail, that's all," said Exp 8, struggling to push the god's foot off him.

"Behold: the Hero of Sel is unable to move! I could crush him at any moment! And if he dies! All of you die!" yelled Etah.

Exp 8 supercharged his jets yet again, sliding out from beneath the powerful legs and then quickly turning around to punch the god's face.

A stray arrow pierced into the gap in Exp 8's arm.

"I told you. I will kill Etah!" yelled the Baroness, ripping out another arrow from her body.

"How are you still alive?" asked Exp 8, rapidly dodging the tyrant's punches with properly timed jet-boosting.

"You know so little." Etah opened his fist and grabbed the hero's head. "Demons don't die, only suffer. Those children you failed to rescue. The ones you saw beheaded before your eyes, they are alive. I don't kill rebels, merely repurpose them! That's what happened with the Baroness! I break wills, not destroy lives. You are fighting to save them from nothing. What will you do now, hero?" asked the Deva, smearing Exp 8 with the blood of the wounded.

The Hero of Sel wrapped his legs around Etah's left arm. "Everyone dies. That's not what I'm against. Everyone suffers. Trying to stop that is pointless. What I fight for…what I died for is freedom! Slavery takes the meaning out of life and the purpose out of suffering! As long as living beings, whether sinners or saints, are trapped in a system of exploitation…as long as willful beings are treated as property, not people, I will keep on fighting! Until the system falls, I will stand and fight!" His jets went into overdrive.

Etah's arm twisted up and then back. The sound of it snapping ringed across the Crimson Coliseum.

Exp 8 careened into the ground and slammed into the wall of the arena.

Etah's left arm shook but he could not raise it.

The people cheered. They climbed out of their seats and charged into the arena, raising their blades, fists, and tendrils as weapons.

"Enough!" Etah's aura burst out from his body, melting anyone who entered it. He stepped up to the defiant hero who was still getting back on his feet.

"The people have stood up to you. You lost. The rebellion won," said Exp 8, gripping one massive orb in between his palms.

"Not another word!" Etah's aura burst out and slammed into Exp 8 from below.

Before the hero could reorient himself, the god gripped his arm.

Exp 8's eyes went blank as his left arm was torn from its socket.

Etah slammed the hero back and forth against the ground by flailing him around by the dismembered arm.

Exp 8's working hand disengaged his grip on the orb. He fell flat on the ground, his palm facing up.

Etah's aura crept out from his feet and held the hero's legs in place.

Exp 8 stood up in a daze, his eyes fixated on the god. His still-attached arm was too weak to form a fist.

Etah's aura shot into the mob. It pulled them in and contorted them into a chair.

The God of Hate created a barrier between him and the mob with his aura. "Listen to your hero now. You'll find his words deficient in valor now that his life is in my hands," said Etah, his aura climbing up the broken mortal's body.

"I can't move," said Exp 8, tears dripping from his helmet.

"Hero. You may live yet." Etah sat down in his living chair and assumed a lax position. "I'm going to give you one chance. Abandon your ideals. Let go of your morals. Stand by my side as a new god of this world. All you have to do to rule alongside me, almost as equals, is lower your head. Bow down to me or perish," he said, staring at Exp 8 with his eyes aflame.

"In that simple gesture lies the injustice of surrender. I will not bow to anyone, neither mortal nor god."

Etah's fiery aura came out from his hand and pressed down on the hero's back.

The Ultimate Exp fought against the weight. He pressed off the ground and looked up at the tyrant, crouched on one knee.

"Ah, much better."

Exp 8 raised his head, his body still held in place by the god's aura. "I will not bow down to you. Even if you break my neck, my willful spirit will wholeheartedly oppose you," said the leader of the Freedom Forcers, his resolve firm and tall like a mountain.

"A fool in the realm of the living and beyond. Such a shame. Your false hope has brought you so much determination, yet in the end, you had to surrender your life to be free."

"I chose to die. I did not surrender. I died for freedom! I am liberated now!" exclaimed Exp 8, raising a defiant trembling fist at the tyrant god.

"Utter nonsense! If you were truly free, you could have chosen to enter the portal of light like you desired. You were brought here by my willpower. Your freedom is an illusion. I own you, body and soul! You do not choose what path you take; I do," said Etah, clenching his fist.

"You may have sent me here, but I choose my path. I also decide what actions I take," said Exp 8, creating an orb in his fist.

Etah snapped his fingers. A figure in a clear cloak came out of the audience and rushed to his side.

"Such a blessed shame! You would have been perfect. You believe in this freedom so fervently you have deceived yourself into thinking you have attained it. Logic and reality have no power over your delusion. It matters not. By opposing me you have become a hero. All sinners, behold: the Hero of Sel stands against me even now! He values your freedom above his own life!"

Sinners throughout the arena raised their fists in solemn silence.

"By refusing me you have created a burning hope. A hope that is inextinguishable no matter what truths ram against it. You are a threat, a true threat. A psychopath who can deny the facts of life can only be tamed with insanity. Soon, you shall become like all the rest here, a brick supporting my foundation. All sinners, behold: I banish this hero to the realm of Absence! When your hero returns, he will be my new footstool!" Etah punched the Hero of Sel, his massive fist a blur.

The legendary leader of the Freedom Forcers was sent flying back. He was gobbled up by an unseen portal and vanished from the Crimson Coliseum.

TO BE CONTINUED IN THE HERO OF SEL RESURRECTION OF THE EXPS BOOK2

NOW AVAILABLE IN EBOOK AND PRINT FORMATS.

SEARCH *HERO OF SEL* @ amazon.com

Also, keep an eye out for the **Comic** in 2020.

RESURRECTION OF THE EXPS BOOK 2 The Hero of Sel. Copyright © 2016 by Alexander J. McCarty

ISBN 978-1-943733-033

If you enjoyed this story then you'll love the ***Of The Exps*** series (3 books currently available in eBook and print form in the link!).

https://amzn.to/2IN29eR

And subscribe to my website too!

https://sphereofcompassion.com

The Main Character!

THE HERO'S EPIC JOURNEY BEGINS!

SEASON 1 PART 1

TRAILER!

Director: Alexander J. McCarty

Editor/Cover Designer: Gabriel McCarty

Seizing the Spotlight!

The Main Character!: The Hero's Epic Journey Begins! Trailer

In times of anarchy, the public often loot and commit violence. Fools. Moments of chaos are opportunity for activists to take action without repercussions.

I find the zoo where all my animal brethren are trapped, but there's someone at the entrance.

"Stand aside or I will cut you down. Those trapped animals will taste freedom today."

"A fellow animal lover," says the man. He rolls up his sleeves and shows me the numbers 7634420. "You think I'd stand guard here during all this madness if I didn't care about them?"

"They deserve freedom."

"These aren't natural animals. GMCs, all of them. They escaped from a testing facility and my boss has made it his mission to provide for them. They wouldn't be able to live in the wild."

I don't have time to waste here. Main is fighting all on his own. And I...I left his side. I need to go to him. He needs his mommy.

"Your boss has created a prison with his compassion. He has no right to take their freedom away." I slice open the doors, creating an opening. "If they want to be here, then they will remain. The choice is now theirs to make."

I run down the streets and spot a familiar face.

Even in a human cesspool of corruption, good people can grow. Banana Man is indeed akin to a water lily.

He waves at me. I spot a figure behind him.

A CatBoy general!

I slice my palms and form kunai as the general's blade comes down on a good person. The general's sword slices into his back as I toss the kunai.

The sword shatters and the general is sliced by my projectiles.

I had feared his life was being turned into a catalyst for Main's character arc. How did Banana man shatter the sword?

Banana Man's coat opens up, revealing a mechanical arm coming from his back. The arm uses the broken sword fragment to parry the next strike.

I join Banana Man's side and form a sword of blood. "Go find your daughter. I'll handle this."

"No. No more heroes are going to die to bring back a girl who doesn't want to come home. The only one going after her is me." Banana man dislocates his joints, becoming taller. His muscles tear his coat apart.

Such power and determination. This man is truly made in the abyss.

"Just decide already. I don't care who I kill first. Oh, pardon my rudeness. My name is CatScratch." The general pulls in the sword fragment and reconnects it to his blade.

"I've decided to bring your daughter back to you, not as a quest but as a duty to a man I respect. You can attack, but only do so when there is an opening. This enemy will not go down easily.

"Neither will I," says Banana Man, spraying the general with a blue fluid.

"***Expel!***" yells the general, sending the fluid off.

Banana Man just gave me the chance to end this.

I bring my sword down on my enemy but it stops in place.

Gravity manipulation, as expected.

Banana Man unfolds a lance and circles around behind the enemy. His jabs are parried by our foe's exceptional sword play.

"My attacks are being pulled into his strikes. I can't get a hit on him," says Banana Man before tossing a flame grenade.

The grenade stops and slams into me.

I use a blood dagger to cut open my right arm. The extra blood lengthens my sword, pressing it into the enemy's chest.

"No! I'm not dying! I am bringing you to Flam!" yells CatScratch, slicing my blood blade and stopping my attack.

"You're loyal to a fault. It will be your undoing. ***Crimson Snake***." My broken sword uses more of my arm's blood and elongates. It twists behind the enemy but is parried.

At least that's what he thinks.

My blood sword coils around his second sword, giving Banana Man the perfect opportunity.

"I'm taking my daughter back from you." Banana Man fires a pistol into CatScratch's head.

"Nooooo!" yells CatScratch

A gravity blast sends me off my feet and smashing into a building.

I've lost a lot of blood. If I don't feed, this body will fail me.

TO BE CONTINUED IN THE MAIN CHARACTER!: THE HERO'S EPIC JOURNEY BEGINS!

NOW AVAILABLE IN EBOOK AND PRINT FORMATS.

https://amzn.to/2ISNoXO

https://sphereofcompassion.com

authoralexandermccarty@gmail.com

https://facebook.com/alexanderjmccarty (Updates often with character art)

http://www.instagram.com/gabriel_of_the_exps

http://www.instagram.com/alexander_j_mccarty

https://twitter.com/of_the_Exps

http://www.tumblr.com/oftheexps

Front Cover design by NobodyMono

https://NobodyMono@facebook/twitter/instagram/tumblr.

https://nobodymono.artstation.com

Back Cover design by Valignar Malrune

https://www.deviantart.com/valignar-malrune

Guardian Angel

Main Character Legendary Origin Stories!

BOOK -1
TRAILER!

By Alexander J. McCarty

Editor/Cover Designer: Gabriel McCarty

Front/Back Art: Cesar Escobar

Chapter 2: Yu-ki the Pacifister

Guardian Angel Trailer

"Stay hidden. I'm going to get you out of here. Oh, and by the way, your hero's name is Yu-ki. That's Yu-ki."

"Yu-ki. We can't leave yet. My sister has been captured and my mom is at the slave auction," I say, tugging at his shirt from inside the basket.

"I just want to get you two to safety. After that, I'm going to free all the slaves," he said, heroism outlining his gentle voice.

I grab my chest.

He's incredible.

"Luna is right down this street. You're going to need help if you want to rescue her," I said, and was given an affirmative "Uhn" by Tumble.

"Fine but if things get crazy, then you leave me behind."

"You're not the boss of me. I bet I'm older than you. I'm sixteen."

"Seventeen," said Yu-ki.

"Wow, you're practically a man." I took in his scent. It was so youthful and strong. Made my head a bit dizzy.

"I think I found the cart. There are seven bandits guarding it. I'm going to set the basket down. Stay inside. I can handle them."

I pop out and leap off his shoulders. "Hey you boys like angels?" I ask, doing a cute pose Mommy taught me where I stick out my butt and put my fingers to my lips.

The human bandits approached and drew their weapons, long metal spears with a hooked tip.

"Wait!" Yu-ki picked up a barrel and set it down in front of them. He then climbed atop it. "These are little girls. By taking them, you're stealing them from their family. Take a moment to think of it from their perspective. I'm assuming some of you have families, maybe a daughter or a sister. What would you do if someone took them away?"

While he distracted them with a speech, Tumble snuck around to the cart and searched for Luna.

"If my daughter sold for as much as she's worth, then I'd sell her myself," said one particularly muscular bandit, stepping out from the crowd.

"Then perhaps we can make a trade. What do you want for the girl in that cart?" Yu-ki took out his satchel.

"Thanks. Saved me the trouble of searching your corpse!" The lead bandit pierced the bag with his spear.

Yu-ki pulled up his shirt as the sleeping gas burst from the satchel. He took me into his arms as my legs went numb.

He had such pretty brown eyes.

Tumble signaled us by hopping up and down.

She found Luna.

Yu-ki danced with one of the limp bandits all the way to the carriage. "See, isn't life more fun when you give instead of take?"

"I will track you down and slice off all your fingers before making you choke on them!" yelled the bandit leader before being dropped.

I hoisted Luna up and had her lean against me.

"Annie?" she asked in a daze.

"Yep. We're going to get you out of here just as soon as we save Mommy!"

"Who's he?" Luna rubbed her eyes.

I jumped up into his arms. "He's my boyfriend."

"Actually, I'm just a hero," he said, scratching his head with blush.

Mmmm. Those flushed cheeks are so tasty looking.

"Awww. He's shy. Yu-ki, admit you're my boyfriend or else I may have to prove it," I said, nuzzling against his chest.

"Annie, focus. The slave auction is being held at the center of the city," said Luna.

"Then why were those bandits taking you out of the city?" asked Yu-ki.

"It doesn't matter. I know where the auction is. You mother, she rescued me from this place. And now she's in danger. Works out fine for me. I get to clear my karma," said Luna, biting into her arm to wake herself up. "Annie, you and Tumble should get in the basket."

"Shouldn't you get a disguise too?" asked Yu-ki.

Luna tore off the cloak of one of the bandits. Her shadow then ripped the bottom part off. She draped it over herself. "I'll hide in plain sight."

I plopped Tumble in the basket before going inside myself.

"Hey, Yu-ki. You better treat my little sister right. If you break her heart, I'll find you and tear out your heart. Got it?"

"You are just adorable. Sorry but threats don't work on me. I'm ready to die anytime anywhere! It's not living life to the fullest that frightens me!"

"Then I'll make you afraid to wake up every morning to a life of constant torture."

"Hey, I'm a nice guy. I mean her no harm."

"Yeah. A bit too nice. Why put yourself at risk to help some strangers? Do you have sisters back home or do you expect some lewd reward? If you want one, then I'll take care of it. Leave the other two out of it."

"Hey, calm down. I'm a loner. And no, I don't have any sisters. I'm an only child. I ran away from home before I was taken to this place. This magical wonderland is where I truly belong," he said, waving to the PorcuPigeons.

"Stop right there," said a voice from in front of us.

I peeked out from beneath the basket and saw a soldier with cat ears.

"You're a hero, aren't you? What are you doing here?" he asks, ready to unsheathe his sword.

"Kitty!" Yu-ki hugs the cat boy soldier.

"I'm not a kitty! I'm a CatKin! Let go of me!"

Yu-ki released him. "Sorry, you just remind me of a cute wittle kitty I met on the street back home."

"Just go on. I've got an important job to do," said the cat boy soldier.

"Stay adorable," said Yu-ki with a salute before heading off.

Luna turned to my hero. "You do realize how dangerous those guys are, right?"

Yu-ki's face darkened and his voice along with it. "Yep. I'm honestly terrified of cats because of them. They wiped out my whole team." He slapped himself and gave a big smile. "Ever since then, I've been a lone wolf. I know how much cats don't like being touched so I thought flustering him would work and, well, it did." Yu-ki opens his palm.

"You stole from a soldier? That's a lot of Cat Coin."

"You shoulda seen what the bandit general was stashing."

"I'm not sure I approve of such a bad boy dating my little sister," said Luna, rubbing his crotch.

"I approve!" I shouted from the basket.

Yu-ki politely moved Luna's hand off him. "Hey, I'm not a thief. I only use money to save lives. I take it from those who would use it for violence and use it to create peace. Oh, looks like we're here."

I stuck my tail out from the basket and looked out with my fourth eye.

Wow. There are so many races gathered. Almost all of them bipedal. Are they all here for the auction?

Yu-ki navigated through the crowd. "Excuse me. Do you happen to know if the mermaid was already sold?"

The hooded man glared at my boyfriend. His entire body was cloaked except his eyes so it was hard to tell what he was. "You know what the real meal is here. The rest of these are just snacks. She'll be up right after this one, but don't expect me to lose to you, little boy."

"I'm seventeen! I'm practically a man."

"You're a boy, young enough for the brothel in town."

"Do you think I'm cute enough?" asks Yu-ki, batting his eyelashes.

The hooded man turned away with a bewildered look.

The speakers blared and my tail eye turned its attention to the podium. The host of the auction was a MounTroll that had priceless minerals in his body instead of regular rocks. "Well, everyone. It looks like we have a tie this round. You know what that means."

"Deal or death!" cheered the crowd.

"That's right. The second highest bidder can use their own bid against the highest bidder. The highest bidder must either fold or accept the challenge."

"Are they going to kill each other?" asked Yu-ki.

The hooded man looked at him, smiling through his mask. "Yeah. It's the entertainment part of the show. If you got the Cat Coin, you can fight me next round. I tend to forget people easily, but I'm sure if I kill ya, I'll remember you just fine."

"I'm flattered. Maybe even a bit excited," said Yu-ki, running his hand up the man's back.

The man took a step back. "If we do fight. Don't do that. Makes me think of my wife. And I come to places like these to forget about her. Oh, the battles about to begin."

"Today we have two legendary bandits pining after the same little Gobli. Who will take home this cute little morsel?" asks the announcer,

"Oh my god, I want to take her home!" squealed Yu-ki.

"Then you better go on up there! I'll watch your cargo," said the hooded man.

"Thankies!" cheered Yu-ki. He put his hand over his face. When he removed it he was harboring an intense glare.

"Excuse me Sir, but you haven't put up a bid yet," said the host.

"That's fine." Yu-ki sliced off the hosts' hand with a super sharp dagger. He then kicked the severed hand into the bidding box. "Consider that my payment."

The host was about to shoot Yu-ki, but the crowd cheered.

"You know, I bet your boss would be mighty impressed if things were a bit more interesting this time," said Yu-ki, shoving a Cat Coin in the host's sever.

"Ladies and gentlemen. It's a two-on-one! Two legendary bandits against this…uh, what are you?"

Yu-ki lifts up his shirt, showing off his sexy thin body. "I'm the Pacifister Yu-ki! Not the best name, but I can't argue with my wanted poster when I look this damn good!" He pulls out a poster from his pants. It's him with his hands posed like a cat and making a silly looking cat face.

"A bounty and a Gobli all in one. My blades sing for your blood," said the crouching two-sworded bandit.

The other bandit simply pointed a single needle at Yu-ki and hissed.

"Luna. What are we going to do? He's going to die," I said, poking her with my tail.

"We wait for the next round and then we get her. Doesn't matter what happens here," said Luna.

Yu-ki spun behind the thin needle wielding bandit and grabbed his arm. He jerked the arm around to deflect the dual sword attack, while backing away. He leaned back to speak to the Gobli in the cage. The Gobli was a little taller than me but I was still way cuter! Her skin was like chocolate and she had long ears that were drooping. The poor girl was draped in rags and bound in chains. "Don't worry. I'll get you home." He said, making her eyes shimmer.

"Looks like he found a new girlfriend," said Luna, sitting on my basket.

"No fair. I saw him first," I said, crossing my arms.

The needle wielding bandit tripped Yu-ki with his foot and flung him over his shoulder.

My hero landed flat on his back and pulled out a big sack when the two bandits approached. "You know what's the best thing about Cat Coin?" asked Yu-ki, tossing one up and down with his thumb.

"It can get you anything?" asks the dual-sword bandit.

"No matter the value, it's all the same size. So, unless you get a really good look, you don't know if three hundred coins are worth three Mews or thirty-thousand!" He swung the sack into the swordsman's weapon and the money tumbled out of it to the ground.

The two bandits dropped their weapons and immediately started shoving as much money into their clothes as possible.

Yu-ki stepped atop them. "Well, looks like I won." He tossed a handful of coins into the host's face and then sliced open the Gobli's cage.

Her eyes lit up with hope once more when he sliced her chains and lifted her onto his shoulders.

"See, isn't this little gift far more precious when she's happy? Look at those sparkling eyes!" Yu-ki leapt back when a dagger was tossed at him from the crowd. "Holy shit! That almost hit me!" he yelled before running off stage with the Gobli.

Luna was giggling. "Wow, you sure found a special hero."

"Yep. I'm gonna make tons of wittle sisters with him!" I exclaimed.

"Annie, you'd be making daughters, not sisters."

"Oh, not sure if I'm ready to be a mommy yet," I said thoughtfully.

The host reattached his hand. "Don't worry everyone. The thief who stole our product will pay with his blood. Anyone who catches him will get his bounty, along with a free annual subscription to our local brother Melting Pot. Now, without further ado, let us bring out the final item on our list!"

Four elves with chained colars brought out a glass encasing. Inside of it was Mommy.

"Luna. What's the plan?"

"The plan was for you to stay home so I could rescue her, but now we simply wait."

"Huh? We can't wait."

"Think Annie. Why storm the auction? We'd only get killed. We just have to follow whoever gets her and kill them. Easy squeezy," said Luna, squeezing my tail.

Is it really that simple? We're going to be a family again super soon!

"You may recognize this fiend from earlier this year. She stormed our auction and stole a ShadowPup from this very stage. This product is a genuine NymphBeast. That's extremely rare! But a full-grown adult like this is an anomoly! The powers of these divine creatures cannot be understated, which is why we have sedated it in a power sealing Goopy. Now, shall we begin the bidding?"

It suddenly started raining, but the rain wasn't coming from above. Instead, water droplets circled around the area.

"We're experiencing some odd weather; let's hurry up with the bidding so we can call it a day," said the host.

The water suddenly expanded, creating puddles across the ground.

"Luna, what's going on?" I asked, poking her leg with my tail.

"I'm not sure," she said.

The hooded man next to us started cackling. "Oh, this is going to be interesting."

Mommy sank inside her tank, seemingly vanishing.

"No magic allowed. If you're caught trying to steal her, you'll not only be killed but you'll be removed from the bandit records!" yelled the host.

Someone screamed in the back, then another. The crowd broke out into a panic.

Are we in danger?

I hugged Tumble close to me inside the basket.

"Your mom sure is amazing," said Luna with a smile.

My tail eye caught sight of her. Mommy would leap out from a pool of water, shoot a concentrated water beam, then ride it and slice through the crowd with her bladed fingers before vanishing into another puddle. She'd pop out, bite into the leg of a bandit and pull him into the puddle as he screamed. Body parts would then appear all around the portals.

Mommy looked so scary.

I covered Tumble's eyes while I gazed at the gruesomely majestic spectacle.

"Your mom's father wasn't a hero, Annie. He was an assassin," said Luna.

"Now what would an assassin be doing with a mermaid?" asked the hooded man.

Mommy popped out of a puddle. Her fangs were gone and she smiled at Luna. "You three didn't have to come all this way. I was captured so I felt I might as well clean out some of the trash before coming home. I'm sorry for worrying you." Her webbed fingers tossed little droplets that loving padded Luna's cheeks.

"Annie and I aren't weak. You have to trust us. We can help too. I want to liberate our people just like," said Luna.

Blades suddenly burst out from Mommy. Her blood sprayed over Luna and the basket.

Mommy. What's going on?

The cloaked man had long tentacles coming out from him, each one with their own weapon.

"Your mission has gotten in the way of progress," said the man.

Mommy turned around and slashed his head with her bladed fingers.

A black vortex was swirling where a face was supposed to be.

"Mommy will be with you all in just a moment," she said before sinking into the puddle.

"Luna! We have to help Mommy!" I yelled.

Luna picked up the basket. "If we want to help, then we'll leave before he decides to take us hostage so he can kill her. Sorry Annie, but that thing is beyond our abilities."

The sound of steam being release suddenly blanketed the area.

"Now what's going on?" I asked.

"No way," said Luna.

I could taste her fear. It made my body feel shaky.

A lance swooped by and sliced open the basket. Tumble and I fell out.

"Target sighted," said a weird creature made entirely from metal. It had an iron helmet and was clad in thick armor plates. An exhaust port came out from its back and released steam.

"What are Anima Collectors doing here?" asked Luna, biting her lip.

"Maybe they're here to help Mommy?" I asked, clinging onto Luna.

"Free merchandise!" yelled some bandits, rushing toward me and my sisters.

"I don't think so!" Luna's shadow picked up some fallen weapons and attacked the bandits.

The hooded man sent his blades at mother, but they missed and went into a puddle.

Mother popped out and shot him with a jet stream before pulling in the blood from the bandits' bodies. Her eyes went red and her whole body sharpened. Bone-like pipes came out from her sides and fired water bullets at the hooded man's tendrils. She then took the blade from a severed tendril and swung it around with her water whip, slicing a bunch of bandits.

Wow! My family is so cool!

"Let them fight. Collect the little ones," said another metal man.

Yu-ki dropped from I don't know where when the metal man approached. His super-heated blade slid down the metal man's swords before chopping off his hand. "Totally robotic which means you don't have a soul. Which also means, I don't have to hold back!" Yu-ki tossed a pouch on the ground that ignited the oil and caused a big boom.

My hero was sent flying back.

I leaped in the way and hit the ground with him. "What's with all those kissie marks on your face?"

"Oh, you didn't know? Gobli's like to mark their mates. She took a real liking to me. Didn't want to say farewell so she marked me for later."

"You're mine," I said, kissing his face repeatedly.

"I'm honestly not sure what's scarier. The horde of heartless machines, the veteran assassin over there, the deadly water goddess, who I'm assuming is your mom, or your persistency," he tapped my nose.

"Can you save Mommy?" I ask.

Yu-ki hopped to his feet and tossed a smoke bomb at the incoming machine men.

"Smoke has no effect on higher beings," said the machine man.

"It's actually a special spice. Smells nice, doesn't it?" asked Yu-ki, sniffing the air.

"I…can't smell."

"Oh, yeah, you're too superior for that. Good for you to since you won't smell that terrible rust."

The machine man's body was rapidly aging and becoming brittle.

"Heathen!" yelled another machine man, using his jets to fly toward my hero.

Yu-ki grabbed the rusting machine and used him to shield the blow. He kicked him and then jumped to the ground with me.

"Why are we ducking?" I asked.

"Oh yeah. I forgot." Yu-ki tossed another satchel that ignited the fire, blowing the two machine men to bits.

"You're amazing!" I leaped into a kiss with Yu-ki. I plunged my tongue deep in his mouth, wiggled it around every corner and even extended it a bit to go down his throat.

A special kiss for my special someone. So happy Mommy taught me how to kiss so good.

Yu-ki's eyes went really wide.

I pulled away and giggled.

"That was…something," he said, blinking repeatedly.

He suddenly dropped me.

That's odd. His arms are still holding me but he's up there.

Blood spurted out from Yu-ki.

Guardian Angel Trailer

A blade zoomed by and went through his legs.

"Shit. I messed up," said Yu-ki, before his torso fell on top of me.

My world went dark. Luna was fighting bandits and Mommy was going up against the man who just killed my hero. I was helpless but to watch.

TO BE CONTINUED IN THE MAIN CHARACTER LEGENDARY ORIGIN STORIES: GUARDIAN ANGEL

NOW AVAILABLE IN EBOOK AND PRINT FORMATS.

https://amzn.to/2N52Wxf

ISBN 978-1-943733-06-4

Published by Sphere of Compassion, Inc.

https://sphereofcompassion.com

authoralexandermccarty@gmail.com

https://facebook.com/authoralexandermccarty

http://www.instagram.com/gabriel_of_the_exps

http://www.instagram.com/sphere_of_compassion

https://twitter.com/of_the_Exps

https://www.tumblr.com/blog/sphereofcompassion

Front/Back Cover Art by

https://www.facebook.com/CesarEscobarArtworks/

Back Cover design by

http://www.instagram.com/gabriel_of_the_exps

About the Author

Alexander McCarty is an animal born on Earth who actively seeks freedom for his fellow animals. He enjoys watching anime, playing video games, reading books by other independent authors, being an activist, writing anime-style stories, and living a vegan life. Having graduated from college with a focus on Asian and Religious Studies, he now spends his time as a writer and as an abolitionist vegan advocate. He listens to any and all comments, suggestions, reflections and criticism.

Please contact me with a link to where you placed a review for any of my books (Of The Exps/ The Main Character) and I will answer any single question as one of my characters for **FREE**. If you do a review (and point out where) in addition to submitting fan art, I will write a **FREE** short 2–4 page story (with my characters) in a scenario of your choosing. =(:3)*

Bloggers who wish to review *Exp 8: Rebellion of the Exps* or *The Main Character: The Hero's Epic Journey Begins Part 1* or *Guardian Angel* may request "Review Copies" at the links below.

authoralexandermccarty@gmail.com

facebook.com/authoralexandermccarty

Fate's Vital Message

Every choice we make has an impact! The animals who are bred to be consumed or turned into clothing are trapped in a Hell without choices. We can cut our connection to their enslavement by living Vegan. Vegan living means abstaining from buying animal products whether they are food, clothing or cosmetic related. It also means not supporting places that exploit animals for entertainment like zoos and aquariums. Create a new future for yourselves and others by living Vegan and inspiring others to follow your ways!

If you need resources, the ones below are the absolute best.

http://www.adaptt.org/

http://www.abolitionistapproach.com/

veganeducationgroup.com

www.ingramcontent.com/pod-product-compliance
Lightning Source LLC
Chambersburg PA
CBHW021244260626
47155CB00004BA/1317